My Captive Highlander

Vonda Sinclair

My Captive Highlander

Copyright © 2015, 2018 Vonda Sinclair

ALL RIGHTS RESERVED

This book may not be reproduced in whole or in part without written permission from the author. This book is a work of fiction. The characters, names, incidents, locations, and events are fictitious or used fictitiously. Any resemblance to actual persons, living or dead, is purely coincidental or from the writer's imagination.

www.vondasinclair.com

ISBN-10: 1981828192
ISBN-13: 978-1981828197

DEDICATION

In memory of my wonderful, loving and encouraging husband. You showed me what a true hero is. I will always love you.

ACKNOWLEDGMENTS

Special thanks to Terry, Dana, Vanessa, Eliza, Judy, Tammy, and Willa.

BOOKS BY VONDA SINCLAIR

THE HIGHLAND ADVENTURE SERIES

My Fierce Highlander
My Wild Highlander
My Brave Highlander
My Daring Highlander
My Notorious Highlander
My Rebel Highlander
My Captive Highlander
Highlander Unbroken
Highlander Entangled

THE SCOTTISH TREASURE SERIES

Stolen by a Highland Rogue
Defended by a Highland Renegade

www.vondasinclair.com

CHAPTER ONE

August 1619

The twenty-oar *birlinn* sliced through the rough waters off Scotland's west coast. The cool wind lashing at him, Shamus MacKenzie glanced up at the dark clouds hovering over the gray-violet sunset. A storm was fast approaching.

His oldest brother, Cyrus, Chief of Clan MacKenzie, had sent him and his two brothers, Dermott and Fraser, along with full crews on their two galleys to escort the Earl of Rebbinglen to Glasgow. Having accomplished their task five days ago, the brothers and clan members were now on their way home. The weather had been calm until this night.

Black clouds rolled in faster and faster. Lightning flashed, near blinding him. They were in for a thrashing.

"Whose canny idea was it to leave Inveraray?" Fraser grumbled behind him.

Shamus turned, barely able to make out his younger brother's blue eyes and black hair in the dimness.

He well knew Fraser would've liked to have stayed at Inveraray for a fortnight with all the lovely ladies. "Cyrus wanted us to return home forthwith," Shamus said loudly enough to be heard over the rising wind. If they'd stayed any longer, no doubt his irritable older brother would've sent a fleet of galleys to fetch them home.

Though now, he wished they had waited a day or two to continue their journey north.

Thunder boomed and the western wind off the sea blasted them. The oarsmen heaved and grunted, trying to stay the course as the galley rode up and down through the giant swells.

"Stay away from the rocks!" Shamus commanded. The white caps and swirling currents betrayed the dangerous hidden boulders closer to shore.

The helmsman shouted something Shamus couldn't hear over the wind.

Drops of rain stung his face, and a moment later, pummeled him in cold sheets.

Saints, he'd never been at sea in such a quick and terrible gale. Blood pounded in his ears as he tried to figure out a course of action. How could he keep his younger brother and his clansmen safe?

Dermott manned the other galley. During a lightning flash, Shamus' gaze scanned over the rough waters and he glimpsed the other vessel some distance behind them.

"May God protect us all," he whispered, salty seawater splashing into his mouth.

Torrents of chill rain drove against them. Though the sail was down, the fearsome wind, along with the enormous waves, propelled the *birlinn* eastward, toward the shore and the treacherous unseen boulders just beneath the churning surface.

"Stay the course!" Shamus commanded, scrambleing over two thwarts and joining the helmsman in the stern. He grabbed hold of the rudder, helping to steer. He squinted through the rain, able to see only the outline of the mainland. The torches on shore they'd been using to help gauge their route had recently been doused in the downpour. The brilliant flashes of lightning revealed little but the violent sea.

A massive wave crashed into the *birlinn* and sent it careening into a deep trough. Shouts sounded all around him as Shamus grappled to keep his hold on the slippery rudder, his stomach dropping.

Was this the end? Would they all die this night?

"Hold on, Fraser!" he yelled.

The oak hull crashed against the rocks and splintered. The massive jolt knocked his hands from the rudder and Shamus plummeted overboard into the icy depths.

Despite the shock, he forced himself to hold his breath, kick his feet and swim toward the surface. Fear for his brothers and the crews of both galleys infused him with strength. Fortunately, most of them knew how to swim, but if some had been hurtled into the rocks, they might be badly injured.

When his head broke through the seawater, he barely had time to inhale before another powerful wave crashed over him, driving him down again. The water roared in his ears. Flailing, he propelled himself to the surface with his legs.

After inhaling a breath of air, he yelled, "Fraser!"

The lightning overhead illuminated naught in the dim gloaming but the giant boulders protruding from the sea. Had their clan's other *birlinn* been smashed to pieces, or had Dermott and the crew managed to stay offshore enough to avoid the peril? Where were Fraser and his own crew?

Shamus flung the wet hair from his eyes and yelled his brother's name again. This time when the lightning flashed, all he saw were fragments of their *birlinn's* broken hull floating out to sea.

"Saints," he hissed. Surely they weren't dead. "Dear God, protect them," he whispered.

Another great wave rose up west of him. He ducked beneath the surface to avoid the worst of the hit. The force of it sent him tumbling deeper. His head and shoulder slammed into a gigantic rock. Pain pounded through him and his head spun. Feeling the boulder anchored in the sea, he climbed up it for a breath of air and held tight. When the next wave struck, he couldn't hold out. The power of it sent him rolling through the waves and all went black.

Maili, younger sister of the MacDonald chief, awoke, gasping for breath in the cool darkness of her bedchamber in Bearach Castle.

Cold seawater had enveloped her. So real. She placed her hands over her head. Nay, her hair was dry.

"Just a nightmare," she whispered, then inhaled sharply and tried to calm her racing heartbeat.

Lightning flared outside and thunder boomed. She leapt up and hurried to her chamber's narrow window. All was dark except when lightning illuminated the loch's rugged and deserted shore line.

Fear iced her veins and she shivered. Someone was out there...in the storm...in the turbulent sea beyond the saltwater loch. His head and shoulder had hit a rock and the pain had been blinding. She'd felt it all as if it were happening to her.

Who was he?

Not one of her kinsmen. Nay, she didn't recognize the man. He was a stranger.

She pressed her eyes closed, once again feeling torn about the special ability she'd possessed since birth. Was it a gift or a curse? Her family hated that she had "the sight" and at times feared her. Even her tyrannical older brother, who had taken over as chief last year when their beloved father had passed, often eyed her warily and gave her a wide berth. Did Elrick fear she would put a curse on him if he didn't please her?

She wished she could, but she knew naught of curses, magic or witchcraft.

What of the man in the sea? Squinting against the bursts of lightning, she sensed nothing from him now. Had he drowned? She couldn't go out to find him, for the storm raged on and her brother's guards would never allow her beyond the gates at this hour. Besides, they would all think her mad.

They did anyway.

Maybe the drowning man had only been a bad dream and not something that was actually happening.

"Please, let it be so," she whispered.

"What is it, m'lady?" her young maid, Anora, asked from her pallet before the fireplace where only the embers glowed.

"The storm awoke me," Maili said.

"Aye, 'tis a bad one."

Maili couldn't stop her eyes from searching the shore every time lightning illuminated it. Someone was out there. She felt him again, as if he were clawing his way from the darkness.

"Do you see something?" Anora asked.

"Nay, 'tis only... I felt something... as if a man were drowning... out there."

"Oh," the maid said in a small voice.

Her strange gift frightened the maids, especially Anora.

Maili wished she could scramble down to the shore and see for herself if a man had washed up, but she didn't ken why she should care. What if he were a dangerous outlaw or pirate? He might kidnap her and hold her for ransom.

Men were a mystery to her. Over the past few years, she'd had three offers of marriage and, after the rumors about her had reached the men's ears, three subsequent rejections. They called her the MacDonald Witch, or the Bearach Witch.

She was no witch; she simply knew things she shouldn't... they claimed. To her, 'twas natural to see things in her mind which were happening at a great distance or in the future, things she could not see with her eyes or hear with her ears. When she'd been a small child, she'd assumed everyone had this ability, but when she'd mentioned it to her nursemaid and her mother, they'd eyed her fearfully.

They always whispered behind her back, but she knew what was in their minds.

A sudden chill gripped her. She hurried back to the bed and crawled beneath the warm blankets. She could not sense the man now. All was empty and dark. Though she didn't know him, she felt hollow inside. How could she miss someone she'd never met?

Distant shouts awoke Shamus. *Where the blazes am I?* When he opened his eyes a crack to the bright sunlight, pain ricocheted through his skull and his whole body. He muttered a curse and tried to make sense of the situation. His plaid and shirt were wet and cold. He lay on an unfamiliar, pebble-strewn beach. Waves crashed nearby.

When he squeezed his eyes closed against the blinding sun, images came to him—the lightning and waves of the storm. The fierce wind. The broken shards of the galley smashed against the rocks.

Fraser? Where was he… and Dermott? And the rest of his clansmen? Shamus lifted his head, wondering if they'd issued the shouts he'd heard. He squinted along the shore and spotted three unfamiliar men swathed in plaids scrambling over the massive boulders and rushing toward him, a sword in each of their hands.

"What the hell?" he muttered and shoved to his feet. The pain that latched onto his left shoulder almost sent him crashing to the ground again. Grinding his teeth, he just managed to stay upright. Blackness threatened. His head swam and he staggered, the pain in it throbbing anew. He grabbed for the sword at his side but it was gone. Damnation, he must have lost it in the storm.

His dirk. His hand closed around the familiar grip. Thank the saints it was still in place. He drew the foot-long weapon from the scabbard. Holding onto a boulder, he tried to take a defensive position against the three warriors advancing on him.

Who the devil were they? And why did they look

like they wanted to kill him?

A dirk against three swords?

'Twas useless. He needed to climb up the cliff farther along the shore. In a limping run, he charged in that direction. After a moment, he glanced back. 'Slud! They were still gaining on him. His toe caught on a stone and he slammed onto the ground. Growling at the pain lashing through him, he grabbed a fist-sized rock and hurled it at his closest pursuer's head. It struck his shoulder and he shouted. His two cohorts rushed Shamus. One kicked the dirk from his hand.

"Who are you, stranger?" one of the men asked, holding the sword's tip too close to Shamus' neck.

"Shamus of Clan MacKenzie. The chief's brother," he said, clenching his teeth against the agonizing pain. Surely they would treat him well if they knew who his brother was. Cyrus held a great deal of power and territory in the northwest of Scotland and the Western Isles. "Our *birlinn* wrecked last night during the storm." He glanced at his shoulder and the torn sleeve of his blood-soaked doublet.

"MacKenzie," one of the men growled as if 'twas a foul word.

"Aye, and if he's the chief's brother…," another said.

Grinding his teeth against the pain, Shamus slowly forced himself to his feet and surveyed the calculating looks on the warriors' faces. Each of them held a sword directed at Shamus.

"I ken all about the MacKenzies." The brown-haired, bushy-bearded man narrowed his eyes. "Your clan killed my father and my uncle at Morar."

"Which clan are you?" Shamus asked, fearing he

already knew the answer.

"MacDonald of Moidart."

"'Twas a battle," Shamus said. "Not murder." Hell, couldn't he have come to his senses anywhere but on MacDonald soil? The MacKenzies and MacDonalds had engaged in a furious feud almost twenty years ago when Shamus was only a lad. The conflict had been a topic much discussed during his childhood. All had been resolved by the king's hand when he'd granted Shamus' father a charter for the land in dispute, and his father had also paid the MacDonalds a large payment.

"Dead is dead," the bearded man grumbled through clenched teeth.

"Not by my hand," Shamus said in a reasonable tone. "Nor did you three kill any of my kin. We were all lads then."

"The chief will want to speak to you," the tall, lanky MacDonald man said.

"Aye, he'll have a cozy, dark chamber for you below stairs." The third man—the one he'd stoned earlier—smirked.

The dungeon? The bastards were going to imprison him. He grabbed for the nearest man's sword arm and gripped his wrist so he'd be forced to relinquish his blade. But, with his injuries, Shamus found his normal strength flagging. They toppled to the ground, pain shooting through him anew. The other two MacDonald clansmen landed blows against his face and chest. Possessed of a sudden fury and survival instinct, Shamus fought them with all his might. When something struck his head, all went black again.

CHAPTER TWO

Maili's hands shook as she tried to concentrate on embroidering green bracken fronds onto a dress, but a feeling of distress near overwhelmed her.

'Twas the same feeling she'd experienced last night when she dreamed of the drowning man.

Maili glanced up at her cousin Constance who sat across from her, embroidering serenely. Fair-haired and green-eyed, Constance was beautiful and she knew it. Maili didn't wish her cousin to know anything about her thoughts. She looked on Maili's "sight" with scorn.

Unable to tolerate the suspense any longer, Maili tossed down her embroidery, sprang from the chair and strode to the window. Her gaze skimmed over the loch, much calmer now in the sunlight and reflecting the brilliant blue sky. At first, she saw naught, then she noticed a small galley being rowed toward the castle. Her brother's scouts patrolled the loch each day and night, going so far as the sea and then returning. Had they picked up the man she'd had the nightmare about?

Her stomach knotted as they rowed closer. When the men leapt ashore and pulled the galley in, one man remained lying in the boat, unmoving.

"'Tis him," she whispered, touching the wavy glass.

"What?" Constance asked behind her.

"Naught."

One of her brother's guards dipped a bucket of water and splashed it into the stranger's face. When he roused, two men dragged him from the boat. The bound stranger was dark-haired, tall and lean... and he wore a tartan weave she'd never seen before.

The two scouts tugged him up the shore and around the side of the castle. He jerked against them, trying to fight or escape. Fury, pain and fear radiated from him.

Who was he and what would her brother do to him? She hastened toward the door.

"Where are you going?" Constance asked.

Maili paused. "Some of the men are bringing in a stranger. I but wondered who he is."

"Why does it matter? Probably someone who trespassed onto clan lands."

"Aye. I'll return forthwith." She calmly exited and closed the door. Once out of sight, she trotted down the narrow stone stairwell to the great hall. She flew down the outside steps just as her brother smashed his fist against the stranger's jaw. *Nay!* One of the other men delivered a fearsome jab to the poor man's stomach. He was already bloody and haggard, his hands bound behind his back.

"Stop!" Maili yelled, racing toward them.

Elrick turned a furious glare on her, his tawny hair glinting in the bright sunlight and his eyes the color of blue flame. "What the bloody hell are you doing out here?"

"Who is he?" she asked. The sight of the newcomer's beaten, battered and bloody face made her ache inside. His doublet was drenched in blood.

When his dark eyes met hers, 'twas clear he was halfway insensible and near to passing out. Something within her demanded that she protect him.

"He's a damned MacKenzie," her brother said. "Why do you care?"

She'd heard about the past blood feud with the MacKenzies years ago. "He's injured."

"Aye, and he's going to be even more injured before I'm through with him." Elrick gave a malicious grin.

Images of war and carnage flashed through her mind. "Nay, you must not harm him further, or you will bring another feud to our clan," she warned.

"Don't think to order me about, sister! Take her inside!"

"What do you intend to do with him?" she asked, trying to keep her voice calm and reasonable.

"Get her out of here. Now!" he ordered.

One of the burly guards picked her up, tossed her over his massive shoulder and carried her up the steps. She pounded her fists against his broad back, fighting to escape, but kept her gaze on the MacKenzie stranger. She had to help him!

But how?

"I cannot wait until she's married and gone from here," her brother grumbled loudly.

Chuckles followed.

"The wee witch is naught but trouble," her brother's sword-bearer and war leader Hamish said.

After the guard carried her into the great hall, the entry door slammed, cutting off the rest of the conversation about her.

"Damn you! Release me!" she told the guard.

He gave a brief laugh and tossed her to her feet.

"Do not place a curse on me, witch. I'm only following orders."

"I am not a witch," she said through clenched teeth and tried to dart around him toward the door.

"Nay." He jumped in front of her and blocked the door.

She hastened across the room to the narrow window that looked out over the barmkin.

Her brother slammed his fist into the MacKenzie man's stomach and he doubled over.

"Stop it, Elrick," she grumbled. Shouting at him would do no good. 'Twould only make him angrier. How could he be so vicious? He was nothing like their dear, departed father or her other brother, Neacal.

Elrick stepped back to converse with three of his advisors. Her gaze locked to the dark-haired stranger. He needed the healer and probably some food. But 'twas something beyond his immediate needs that drew her attention. Something that made her want to run to him and protect him against her own clansmen.

She sensed he was a man who would be important to her.

As Shamus stood in the walled barmkin, pain lacerated every part of his body. He ground his teeth to keep from groaning and showing weakness before these bastards. He blinked, trying to maintain full awareness.

The chief and his men talked of ransom and how much they could get for him. If that was what they intended, they wouldn't kill him at least. But they wouldn't care how many injuries they gave him on top of the ones he'd endured in the ocean.

His throat dry as sunbaked sand, he swallowed and tried to remain still as he puzzled over why the chief's sister had come to his defense with such vehemence. They'd called her a witch. Could it be true? One thing was certain, her lustrous dark hair and fair face were the only rays of hope and beauty at Bearach Castle.

"Take him to the dungeon," the young MacDonald chief commanded. The whoreson appeared younger than Shamus' own twenty-eight summers.

When he didn't move fast enough, the two clansmen dragged him by the arms. Pain stabbed through his shoulder.

"Bastards," he growled as they pulled him toward a doorway.

In retaliation, they yanked on his injured shoulder extra hard. Once in the dungeon, they cut the ropes binding his wrists, tossed him onto the hard-packed dirt floor of the cell and slammed the iron door shut. Pain smashing through several parts of his body, he lay still, his teeth clenched tight, praying the agony would go away.

What the devil had he done to deserve this?

The aches wracking his body eased away bit by bit in the silence after the men left. He inhaled a deep breath of the dank, mildew-scented air and opened his eyes. The only weak light came from a torch in the stone corridor farther along.

Where were Fraser and the rest of his clansmen? Had they survived the galley wreck or were they all dead, drowned, and washed upon some other clan's shore? And what of Dermott, his crew and galley?

Shamus' stomach ached with fear for his brothers. The pain in his head throbbed so severely, nausea rose up within him. At the same time, his mouth felt parched and dry as a ten day old bannock.

How long would they leave him here? And how would they get word to Cyrus that he was being held? He hoped they would send a messenger soon.

"Tavia, gather your supplies," Maili whispered to the clan healer a short time later, then glanced over her shoulder at those in the great hall. Neither her brother nor his closest men were present and it was not yet time for midday meal. "We must see to the stranger's injuries."

"Who is he?" Tavia asked, keeping her voice equally quiet. Though she was more than a decade older than Maili, they had been close since Maili had broken her arm as a wee lass and Tavia had set it.

"The MacKenzie chief's brother. A gentleman of the clan. If Elrick kills him or injures him further, I fear what the MacKenzies will do. Come down on us with fire and sword, without doubt."

Tavia lifted a mischievous brow, her green eyes twinkling. "Are you certain that's the only reason you wish to help him? Or is there something else?"

Maili frowned. "Is that not enough?"

"Of course." Tavia grinned. "But I'm thinking you're drawn to the mysterious stranger."

"Well..." Maili rolled her eyes. "I could not even tell if he was handsome or not, with his face so swollen and bloody," she said, trying to pretend she had no interest in him. "His shoulder was bleeding badly. While you're preparing your herbs and supplies, I'll go fetch him some food from the kitchen."

"Are you sure the chief will allow us into the dungeon to help him?"

"If he does not, I'll appeal to the elders and the council."

A portion of the clan was already dissatisfied with Elrick's leadership skills, or lack of them. He was too hotheaded and impulsive, they said. 'Twas sad her other brother, a year younger than Elrick, had left the clan several months ago. She did not even ken whether Neacal was still alive. Every day, she prayed he was, for she missed him. He had always treated her with kindness. He had a dark and tormented soul and could not abide the castle walls. He'd told her he had to leave to save his own sanity.

After gathering a few bannocks and a jug of ale for the stranger, along with a woolen blanket for warmth, she met Tavia in the great hall and they proceeded out to the sun-warmed bailey where a high, thick stone wall surrounded them. Lifting the hem of her plaid *arisaid*, she stepped over a puddle of water which remained from last night's storm as they strode toward the entrance to the dungeon.

"We've been sent to see to the prisoner's injuries," Maili told the two guards.

The massive guard, Gegrim, wearing leather armor and helm, crossed his arms over his chest. "The chief mentioned naught to us about it."

"What are you about, Maili?" Elrick yelled as he crossed the courtyard.

Stiffening her spine, she waited until her brother stopped a few feet away. "We're trying to make sure your prisoner survives. What do you think the

MacKenzie chief will do if his brother dies here at your hand?"

"Not at my hand, my daft sister. He was already badly injured when my soldiers picked him up."

"Do you think the MacKenzies will believe that?" she challenged.

Elrick narrowed his eyes. "I don't give a damn."

"I'll ask the elders what they think we should do, then," she said.

"Nay, not a word to them," Elrick growled. "Go. See to the whoreson, and be quick about it." He turned to the guards. "Watch them and make certain the prisoner does not escape."

Gegrim gave a sharp nod and stepped aside. Maili proceeded down the stone steps into the darkness below, Tavia following.

Good lord, how Maili hated the dungeon. She could distinguish little until Gegrim brought forth a torch. Then she saw that the prisoner lay on his side on the filthy dirt floor of the cell. The second guard unlocked the door and she entered with Tavia.

"We need better light," Maili said, motioning Gegrim forward. He entered the cell and stood near them, bringing the torch so close the heat of it warmed her skin.

Maili knelt on the floor beside the dark-haired man. "Master MacKenzie, we're here to dress your wounds. And we brought food."

He turned his bloody face toward her and his swollen eyes opened a crack. "Thirsty," he whispered.

"Of course." Damn her brother and his men for beating him so badly. "I have some ale," she said in a soothing voice. After uncorking the stoneware jug, she tilted it to his mouth. He drank heartily, some of the liquid running down his cheek and spilling onto the floor.

He lay back, breathing hard. "I thank you, m'lady," he whispered.

"What is your name?" Maili asked.

"Shamus MacKenzie." His voice was a bit stronger, not as raspy.

"I brought the healer to tend your wounds. Are you in much pain?"

When he didn't answer, she grew concerned. "Master MacKenzie—"

"Shamus," he murmured.

"You will not harm us, will you, Shamus?" she asked.

"Nay."

Kneeling, Tavia set about removing his doublet and shirt while Maili stood beside the guard holding the torch and tried not to watch. But Shamus was a lean and finely-hewn man with broad shoulders and defined muscles in his chest and arms. She had accidentally glimpsed a few men of her clan, distant cousins, taking swims in the loch at sunset once but none would compare to Shamus.

The healer cleaned the wound on his shoulder and rubbed healing salve on it before bandaging it. Once she was done, she helped him put on his shirt and doublet again. Next, she cleaned the cuts and bruises on his face and head, then smoothed the salve on them.

For once in her life, Maili envied the healer, for she had good reason to touch him. Maili had never wished to touch a man before, nor even be near one.

"There we are, sir," Tavia murmured and arose from her knees. She then took the blanket Maili had brought and covered him with it.

"I appreciate it," he said.

Maili moved forward. "Would you like to eat? I brought bannocks."

"Aye." He turned onto his side, facing her.

She dug into her satchel, crouched and handed him the oatcake.

"I thank you." His raspy voice grew stronger. "You are the chief's sister, are you not?"

How had he figured that out? From her and Elrick's argument in the barmkin earlier?

"Indeed."

When he finished the bannock in three bites, she handed him another one. He must surely be starving.

"How long since you've eaten?" she asked.

"I know not. 'Haps a day."

With his injuries, 'twould be best if he didn't overeat at this meal.

Though she wished she could stay longer, she feared 'twas time for her and Tavia to take their leave. "Do you have need of aught else?" she asked him.

"Aye, my freedom."

Well, of course. If only she could grant that to him, she would. She arose, stepped back and glanced at the scowling guard who held the torch.

"Can you arrange it?" Shamus asked.

She couldn't believe the slight grin on his swollen lips. Was he mad?

"Nay, I fear not."

"A pity," he mumbled.

Saints, but he was a teaser. How she wished she could've met him under far different circumstances. Regret tensing her muscles and her stomach in knots, she moved toward the cell's door and prayed her brother would not kill him before he gained his freedom.

CHAPTER THREE

Shamus slept, he knew not how long. The loud clanging of metal awoke him. He squinted at the bright torch outside the cell's bars.

"Wake up, Laird MacKenzie! I have your supper feast." The guard dropped something onto the ground, turned and left him in near darkness.

Bastard! Shamus couldn't believe he was in the MacDonald clan's dungeon. He ground his teeth against the soreness slicing through his body at the least movement.

He must have slept for several hours for he was again hungry. He forced himself to endure the agony of getting to his feet. His head throbbing, he swayed, limped to the iron bars and crouched.

Expecting the worst—moldy bread and rotting meat—he untied the worn cloth bundle to find a generous amount of fresh bread and cheese and a skin of ale. Pleasantly surprised, he smiled. Had the lady prepared this for him? He wished she would've brought it to him.

He devoured it, thankful he had good food at least.

After eating, he tested the strength of the iron bars, as well as that of the door. Neither budged. "Damned MacDonalds," he muttered. Except for her, of course, and her healer.

The lady was a wee fae creature with dark hair and wide-set pale eyes. He guessed they must be blue or green, though 'twas hard to tell in the torchlight.

How soon would the chief send his messenger to Cyrus? He hoped 'twas soon. Cyrus would be furious with the MacDonalds, and with Shamus, too, for getting himself into this fix.

What about Fraser and the rest of his crew? He prayed they had not drowned. Surely, if they'd washed up on shore alive, the MacDonald scouts would've brought them in and imprisoned them, too.

Prior to this, he had never been to this castle and didn't know how strong their defenses were. The walls he'd glimpsed when they'd hauled him in appeared to be thick and well repaired.

The chief's sister haunted him... her image teased at his overburdened mind. What was her name? Mayhap he could convince her to secretly help him escape. There had to be some way out of here.

Pains shot through his left shoulder, and his head ached with a dull throb. Thankfully, his legs hadn't been injured, just a few scrapes and bruises from bumping against the rocks in the ocean. And his sword arm was still good. If he could get out of this hell-pit, he could travel north on foot, or mayhap find someone with a galley to take him back to Dornie.

Could he convince the lass to help him? Would she even visit him here again?

※

Hours later, voices echoed from some distant part of the dungeon. Shamus opened his eyes to see light from a torch barely illuminating the darkness. How long had he slept? Was it night or day?

When he turned onto his back, soreness shot through his muscles like sharp arrows. He gritted his teeth and suppressed a groan.

"Have you checked on him?" asked a female voice. 'Twas her. The fae lass.

"Nay," growled the guard as they descended the steps.

Lying still and pretending sleep, Shamus squinted, watching as they approached the cell door.

The guard shoved the torch into a wall sconce and turned to leave.

"Unlock the door," she said.

"Nay. The chief said you are not to go inside." He clomped away.

"Bastard," she hissed in a low whisper as she stared after the guard. When a distant door slammed, she turned her attention back to him. "Sir? Shamus… are you awake?"

"Aye." Clenching his teeth against the pain, he pushed himself to a sitting position.

"And how are you feeling this morn?"

'Slud, that much time had passed? "As if I was trampled by a herd of red deer," he grumbled, trying not to let her see exactly how much he hurt.

"The guard won't let me in to check your wounds."

"I heard."

"Are you able to rise to your feet and come over here to the bars? I've brought you food to break your fast. I wanted to return last night but Elrick wouldn't allow it. Did you get the food I sent?"

"Aye and I appreciate it."

He could understand her brother not allowing her to return. Shamus certainly would've never allowed his sister, Isobel, to visit a prisoner without a guard present.

The MacDonald chief was a damnable tyrant, but still not half as formidable as Cyrus. His brother would chew the whoreson up and spit him out first chance he got.

Trying not to groan, Shamus slowly pushed himself to his feet and straightened. His head and shoulder pained him greatly. When a wave of dizziness struck, he grabbed onto one of the iron bars, thankful his sword arm was uninjured.

"Here are three bannocks." She offered them to him through the bars.

"You are too kind." He accepted the oat cakes and took a bite. He savored the freshly baked, buttery flavor.

She turned her head sideways, trying to view his shoulder injury in the low light where his doublet and shirt were torn. "The bandage is bloody again. I must have the healer return."

"'Tis healing," he muttered between bites. At least he hoped it was. He needed to be out of here and away. Never had he been imprisoned in a dungeon before. "But I would appreciate it." He would accept any hospitality she was willing to offer, and mayhap he could devise a way to escape.

She eyed his face carefully. Damnation, but she was a beauty, her creamy skin taking on a golden glow in the torchlight. Her pale blue eyes were bewitching and almost mystical. Though she wore the cowl of her *arisaid* over her head, some of her loose midnight hair draped forward. But her lips... saints... they were dark and luscious like a ruby bow.

As for himself, he well knew he looked atrocious, for one of his eyes was still swollen almost shut. His face felt as if it were covered in bruises where her brother and his men had beaten him.

Looking as he did, he could never seduce his way out of here. Still, she did seem incredibly concerned about him.

After finishing the last bite of the bannocks, he swallowed. "I thank you for the food." The more he moved, the more the pain in his limbs abated. Even his head felt clearer. Aye, movement was what he needed.

"I brought ale, too." She held up a stoneware jug decorated with the face of a bearded man, vines and leaves.

"'Twill not fit through the bars."

"You will have to drink from here." She tilted the jug up to the bars.

He moved closer, placed his mouth against the lip of the jug and drank. He enjoyed the warm and nurturing feeling that spread over him because she gave him ale this way, similar to feeding him by hand.

He drank deeply, not realizing how thirsty he'd been. "'Tis good." He drank the rest of it, then swallowed.

She placed the jug on the floor.

"What is your name?" he asked.

She glanced toward the steps, then back to him. "Maili," she whispered.

'Twas a sweet name that fit her. He wanted to grin at her charming mannerisms, as if she wished no one to ken she'd told him her name... as if it were a secret between them.

He observed her closely, the concerned look in her eyes riveting him. What in blazes was going through her head? 'Twas clear to him that she had a keen, intelligent mind.

Could he convince her to help him escape?

If he did, he might be putting her life in danger, too. What would her brother do to her if he learned of it?

Saints! Don't even think of it. She'd helped him already by bringing him food, drink and seeing to his wounds. He couldn't do anything to endanger her.

Heavy footsteps pounded down the stone stairs. Maili spun around and drew back. She was jumpy. Did she fear her own clan?

The chief came into view in the torchlight, followed by one of his bodyguards.

"I thought I saw you sneak down here," he said to Maili in a snide tone.

"I did not sneak, Elrick," she said firmly. "You gave me leave to bring your prisoner food."

"Aye, and how is our esteemed guest faring?" Elrick observed Shamus, mockery glinting in his eyes.

Shamus wanted to punch the bastard in his smirking mouth.

"If you wish a large ransom, he will need to be in good health," Maili said.

"I can see that he is. I've sent messengers to Teasairg Castle with my terms written out."

"When?" Shamus asked, trying to keep his fury under control until he was free and had a weapon.

"This morn."

If the weather was good, and they had a fair wind, they would reach Dornie by galley in a day or two. Cyrus would take immediate action. 'Haps in four or five days he could be out of this hell-pit.

He glanced at Maili and her worried frown. What did it mean? Was she terribly concerned about him being locked up or did something else trouble her?

"Fatten him up, Maili. We want him looking bonny when his brother arrives." Elrick chuckled. "Now go." He motioned her toward the stairs. "We'll have guests arriving soon and you need to see they are well cared for."

Maili narrowed her eyes, irritation tightening her features, but she did not argue with her brother. She slid Shamus one last glance and headed up the steps.

Elrick took the torch and followed, leaving Shamus in darkness.

Although Elrick had prevented Maili from spending more time with Shamus, at least he'd allowed the healer to see to his wounds again and change the dressings. Maili spent the day directing the servants and overseeing preparations for food and sleeping quarters for their distant MacDonald cousins, a different branch of the clan from Skye, who would arrive shortly. Her brother said it was not unexpected. He had asked Chief MacDonald of Sleat to visit to discuss clan affairs. She had seen the bearded, graying chief before, several times during clan gatherings and such.

When the lookouts announced they'd spied the fleet of galleys approaching from across the loch, Maili changed into her nicest gown, embroidered with roses and leaves.

When Sleat and his men arrived in the great hall,

she welcomed them as warmly as possible and tried to ignore Chief Sleat's rude and assessing stare. His behavior was not surprising. Anyone who had heard the witchcraft rumors gawked at her unabashedly.

She stepped aside and motioned them toward the high table.

"'Tis nice to see you again, lass," Sleat said, sidling up to her. Before she could move out of his way, he grabbed her derriere and squeezed.

Gasping in shock, she elbowed him upon impulse. *Bastard!*

He chuckled and proceeded toward the table.

Ugh! She cringed. What on earth? She would definitely have to steer clear of that old goat. As soon as the men were seated, she directed the maids to serve supper.

She sent another glare Sleat's way. He was about the age of her father. A blade of sadness struck her. How she wished Da was here now. She missed him sorely. After her mother had passed when she was a wee lass of six summers, her da had always given her extra attention and carried her around on his shoulder. And he'd always told her she was bonny like her dear mother.

"Come, sit at the table with us, Maili," her brother called and motioned to her.

Blast! She had hoped the men would ignore her so she might slip away, once the meal was underway, and visit Shamus.

Reluctantly, Maili stepped onto the dais and took the empty seat beside her cousin Constance who was animated and smiling at all the male attention directed her way. Aside from the two of them, all those at the high table were men. Many of them continued to watch Maili openly and with suspicion. Were they curious about the Bearach Witch? Did they fear she would put a curse on them?

"Your sister has grown into a beauty, Elrick," Sleat said.

Maili frowned at the older man, but he sent her a tight-lipped grin, lust gleaming in his eyes.

She stifled a shiver and focused on her food. 'Twas not the first time a man had remarked on her looks, but Sleat usually ignored her. What possessed him this day?

Elrick changed the subject to clan affairs, which she was glad for.

She ignored the men as best she could and ate, allowing her mind to wander to Shamus.

He was not an outlaw and should not be imprisoned. He'd done naught wrong. She wished she could go visit with him again after supper, but she feared Elrick or his guards would stop her.

A vision flashed in Maili's mind of another clan attacking their castle. Steel clanged and blood puddled in the courtyard. She jumped, her eyes flying wide as she glanced around the table. Several of the men noticed her abrupt movement and gave her curious stares. Nay, 'twas not their distant kin who would attack, but strangers…the MacKenzies, intent on rescuing their brother.

Horror and nausea ripping through her, she leapt up from the table. "Pray pardon." She rushed across the great hall and up the steps to her bedchamber.

She barred the door and shook her head, trying to clear it of the ghastly images of war and death. 'Twas her own clan who would suffer. How could she stop it?

After adding peat to the fire, she paced before the hearth. Elrick should not hold Shamus for ransom. He would regret it. How could she convince her brother to release him? He would not see reason. The glint of gold had blinded him to the truth.

A quarter hour later, a knock sounded at the door. When she opened it, a female servant stood outside. "The chief wishes to see you in the library."

Good. Now would be a perfect opportunity for Maili to tell him what an idiot he was... well, not in those words, but something close to it.

When she entered the library and closed the door, Elrick turned from the fireplace. "Why did you act like a madwoman during supper?" he demanded.

"What?" She halted abruptly, surprised at his blunt question. "I did not."

"You jumped up and fled as if you feared our cousins."

"Nay, 'twas not that. I do not fear them."

"What then?" Elrick's frown remained in place.

"Naught." Maili could think of no convenient lie to cover her odd behavior. In the past, several of Maili's premonitions had come to pass, but because she'd kept most of her visions secret—to avoid being ridiculed—she had no proof. In her visions, she had perceived that if something changed, the outcome would change too.

"I will have an explanation from you now," he ordered.

She stiffened her spine. "Very well. If you wish the truth, I had a vision."

He rolled his eyes and blew out a long breath. "You ken I don't believe in that rubbish. What sort of *vision* did you have this time?"

"We're going to be attacked. You should not be holding Master MacKenzie for ransom."

"Why would the MacKenzie chief endanger his brother's life by attacking? He has more gold and silver than he can spend in his lifetime. He will not miss a few thousand pounds. Aside from that, my men are highly trained."

"Regardless, our clan will suffer greatly from this attack. Many MacDonalds will be killed."

"Are you questioning my leadership skills, my training skills?" he growled.

"Nay, 'tis only—"

"I want to hear no more about it! You will act like a normal woman from now on or you will regret it."

CHAPTER FOUR

The next morn, Shamus heard light footfalls padding down the stone steps along with the clunking ones of the guard who carried a torch. Was Maili coming to visit him? He sat up and waited, happy when her sweet face came into view. He was surprised he could discern her footsteps from others.

He arose to meet her at the iron bars. The pain in his body had diminished considerably, though his injured shoulder and the lump on his head were still sore. Still, he hardly felt them, for the grin Maili tried to hide captured his full attention.

After the guard secured the torch in the sconce, he disappeared up the steps. Coming forward, Maili handed Shamus a cloth bundle and the scent of warm bread and something sweet and buttery reached his nose. It smelled luscious.

"Mmm, what treat do you have for me this morn, Lady Maili?"

She tried to hide her smile but he caught it, along with the twinkle in her eye. He thought 'haps she liked him a wee bit—he hoped—despite his battered face. At least the swelling in his eye had shrunk a great deal.

He unwrapped the parcel to find two warm buttery scones filled with wild strawberry preserve. He did not think her brother knew of her squandering such valuable food on a prisoner. With relish, he bit into the confection, the likes of which had no equal. He moaned in pleasure at the mouthwatering flavor. He ate slowly, savoring each morsel, while feasting his eyes upon Lady Maili's lovely face. He would swear she was blushing, though 'twas difficult to tell in the dimness... and she seemed hesitant to meet his gaze.

Though this imprisonment was one of the worst experiences of his life, he treasured these fleeting moments with Maili. She would never know how much her visits meant to him.

He swallowed the last bite. "'Twas the most delicious thing I have thus far tasted." But he had a feeling her lips would be far more delectable... if he ever had an opportunity to kiss her.

"Our cook has no equal."

"Indeed. So, who are your visitors?" he asked, curious since last night about whether the newcomers were friends or foes of the MacKenzies and whether they might help him gain his freedom.

"Distant MacDonald cousins from Isle of Skye."

"Sleat?" he guessed.

She lifted a brow. "How did you know?"

Disappointment engulfed him. "Our clan's castle, Teasairg, is not too far from Isle of Skye and Sleat's holdings." The MacKenzies tolerated Sleat. That was the extent of it. No fondness existed between them. The MacKenzies were always vigilant about a potential attack from their neighbor. And they would certainly be of no help to him here.

"I brought your ale in this wine bottle. 'Twas the only thing convenient about. The kitchen servants are in a stew with all the guests." She removed the cork and handed the bottle to him. He took it, unable to believe she would give him something he could easily use as a weapon. She wasn't daft, so... did she trust him that much? If that was the case, he was thrilled. He turned up the bottle and took a long swallow.

After glancing behind herself, she moved closer and whispered, "I wish there was something I could do to help."

He searched her face. 'Twas too much to hope for. "What do you mean?"

She fidgeted. "I... I don't know. I only know that my brother should not be holding you prisoner."

"I most heartily agree, but why do you say that?"

"You are not a bad man or an outlaw."

He suppressed a smile. Of course he wasn't, but how did she know that? They had talked a few times, but she barely knew him. Could he trust her?

"My brother is going to bring destruction to our clan unless..." She snapped her lips shut and glanced down.

"Unless what?"

She shook her head. "Elrick said he will ask a high ransom for you because your brother has plenty of funds. I told him 'twas a mistake to ask for any ransom."

Shamus was stunned for a moment. "Indeed?"

She nodded.

"You are a brave lass to speak so to the chief."

She shrugged. "My brother has been daft the whole of his life."

Shamus tried to lift a brow, but it hurt too much. He suddenly found himself wanting to know more about her and her family. "Do you have more brothers? Sisters?"

"Aye, I have another older brother who is a year younger than Elrick."

"Is he daft as well?"

"Nay." She frowned and a shadow passed behind her eyes. "He is..." She shook her head. "I shouldn't speak of it."

"Why? Does he live?"

Maili's troubled gaze met his. "Aye, as far as I know, but he left the clan."

"Why?"

"I know not the entire story." She glanced away.

He had to keep her talking somehow, get her to trust him. Then, mayhap she would help him... if she knew more about him. Although... he still felt conflicted about putting her in danger. "I have four brothers and a sister," he said. "I'm the middle one."

"'Tis a large family, larger than mine at least. Do all of you live at your clan's castle?"

"Aye, all except for my sister, Isobel. She married the MacKay chief last year and they live on the north coast."

"I wish I had a sister," Maili said wistfully. Had she been lonely as the only girl? "What are your brother's names?"

"Cyrus is the oldest, then Dermott. Fraser is three years younger than I am, and Liam is the youngest." He wanted to tell her that Fraser had been in the galley wreck with him, but he was still unsure whether he could trust her entirely. If she happened to tell her brother, he might send men out looking for Fraser and the rest of the crew. He prayed Fraser was alive and well. Dermott, too, of course. He missed them both. He had to find his way out of the dungeon as soon as possible so he could search for them.

"Are they all married?" she asked.

"Nay, none of them are as of yet."

"Why?"

"Well, Cyrus should be the one getting married first," Shamus said. "After all, he's the Lord of Kintail and the chief. He will need an heir. He's been contemplateing his options for a couple of years. He wants to secure the best possible clan alliance. I'm thinking he is hoping for an earl's daughter."

"I see."

"Dermott is second in command and the tanist. He has no reason to marry at the moment." Nor did Shamus or his other two brothers. Fraser and Liam were both too young anyway, still sowing their wild oats. Fraser in particular chased after every pretty lass he caught sight of.

"Elrick is the same, hoping to marry and obtain a beneficial clan alliance."

Shamus nodded. "What of your clan's council? Do they support your brother's decisions?"

"The elders disagree with him about holding you hostage. I overheard them discussing it in secret."

Shamus saw a glimmer of hope. "Mayhap you could talk to them and see if they would sway his decision."

She watched him with trepidation. "I will try, but they rarely listen to me. What will your brother do when he learns of your capture?"

Shamus didn't wish to frighten the lass, so he wouldn't tell her the whole truth. Cyrus could be volatile, as well as cold and ruthless when one of his family members or friends was threatened. Who knew what he would do?

"To be honest, I don't ken. He's unpredictable,"

Shamus said.

"Well... I ken." She dropped her gaze. "I have seen."

Perplexed, Shamus frowned. "What have you seen? Have you met my brother?"

"Nay." She stepped away from the bars. "I must go now."

"Wait." Did she have the sight? He remembered that her brother's men had called her a witch when they'd first brought him in. "Are you a witch?" he asked.

She frowned. "Nay! I am not." She turned and hastened up the stairs.

Hell, now he had made her angry.

"Pray pardon," he whispered to the echoes of her retreating footsteps. He hadn't meant to insult her. He respected those who had second sight and thought it must be a grand gift.

She was an unusual lass, one such as he'd never met before. What had she meant? Had she seen into the future?

In his hand, he still held the wine bottle containing a bit of ale. He drained it and imagined the bottle as a weapon. Aye, 'twould be a good one.

"I would have the bottle back, if you don't mind," Maili said the next day when she brought Shamus his midday meal. Blast him! He had called her a witch. Was he like everyone else?

He moved to the bars. One of his eyes was still a wee bit swollen. But by torchlight, she could now see that his eyes were a rich, gleaming brown and that he was a most beautiful man, despite the bruises which remained on his face.

"Maili, I'm sorry I asked if you were a witch. I meant no insult."

His words shocked her and she stepped back, searching his face. Did he mean it?

"No harm done," she muttered, wishing to change the subject as soon as possible. "About the bottle..."

"Which bottle?" The knave eyed her innocently.

Maili placed her hands upon her hips. "You know perfectly well which bottle. The one I allowed you the use of yesterday. If you do not give it back to me, I'll not bring you any more ale."

"Och. You're a brutal lass." He tried to hide his smile.

"I am not bluffing."

The corner of his lips quirked up. "I dropped it and broke it. My swollen and injured fingers, you see." He held up his hand for her inspection.

His hand didn't look injured. She narrowed her eyes and tapped her foot, not believing him for an instant. "Let me see the bottle."

"I tossed it into the corner so no one would cut themselves on it. I don't wish you to carry it. You could injure yourself."

"If the guard or my brother find out I gave it to you, they'll have my head."

His entire demeanor switched from playful to serious. "In truth? Your brother would do that?"

"Nay, probably not, but he'll lock me in my chamber and not allow me or anyone to bring you more food. And if you wish this fresh bottle of ale I brought, you'll have to give me the broken one."

He let out a long breath. "Very well. Give me a

piece of cloth and I'll wrap the broken shards of glass in it. You can take it safely out that way."

She handed him an old piece of plaid. He crouched in the corner, and the pieces of glass tinkled together as he piled them onto the cloth. He had told the truth... but had he broken the bottle in order to use a shard of glass as a blade on one of the guards?

The bundle secure, he handed it to her. She then gave him the wooden bowl of warm venison stew.

He sniffed. "Nice reward." He eyed her intently. "I wish we could eat supper together at a table," he said, then took a bite.

Wishing the same, she tried not to stare at him. She was coming to appreciate his tall, lean and muscular frame. Each day the handsomeness of his face became more and more evident to her as the swelling went down and the bruising lightened.

"You are very generous to bring me venison stew." He held the wooden bowl in his hand and scooped out a large bite.

She wanted him to heal and regain his strength before his brother arrived to pay his ransom—or attack. She wasn't certain what the outcome would be. Different scenarios played out in her head each night as she tried to sleep. Sometimes she could see into the future and sometimes she could not. Much depended on the decisions of everyone around her.

"Do you like the stew?" she asked.

"Aye, 'tis delicious." With dark eyes, he observed her closely... too closely, then gave her the empty bowl.

She handed him a fresh bottle of ale through the bars.

She watched his throat work as he drank long

swallows. Once the bottle was empty, he eyed it, then smiled at her.

She reached a hand through the bars. "I would have it back now." Her words were only slightly less than a demand.

"Would you now?" He raised a dark brow, a wee grin playing upon his enticing lips.

"Shamus," she warned.

"Maili." His sensual voice caressed her name in an inviting manner. He took her hand and lifted it. When his warm lips touched her skin, a shocking and thrilling tingle shot up her arm and throughout her entire body.

She jerked her hand away. What was that? Magic, a spell? Never had a man's touch sent such a startling reaction through her. Not that many men had touched her, but a few had kissed her hand.

"Do not tease me," she said, trying to regain her bearings. "You well ken you cannot keep the bottle. I've only finished telling you why. They'll not let me bring you more food."

"I'll give it to you if…"

She waited a long moment for him to finish. "If what?"

"If you give me something in return."

Heat stole over her for she suspected he might be trying to charm her, and she was not immune. 'Twould be too easy to fall under his spell. "I've already given you food. You are mighty demanding for a prisoner."

A grin quirked his lips. "There is something I want from you after I'm free."

She was afraid to ask, but she had to know. "And what is that?"

"A kiss."

Scorching heat rushed through her. How could he say such a thing to her? A kiss? Oh, aye, 'twould be a most heavenly experience.

"And, of course, I'll return the favor," he said. "I want to give you a kiss to thank you for helping me heal and for feeding me when your brother would have forgotten me down here and allowed me to starve."

"Nay," she blurted, though she wanted to grab him through the bars and kiss him now. But what if he was only attempting to charm her to get his way? She had to stay focused on her main concern—the clan and their safety.

"Nay?" he asked, lifting a brow subtly.

"Exactly. I refuse." She crossed her arms over her chest, trying to appear more resolute than she felt.

"Why?"

"If your brother is as ruthless as I'm imagining, none of us MacDonalds may be alive after he learns you're here. He may storm the place and exercise the power of fire and sword against us all."

Shamus shook his head. "He doesn't kill women and children, only armed enemy soldiers."

"Well, that's one good thing, I suppose," she whispered. Though she didn't want to see her male clansmen lying dead either.

"I wouldn't let him hurt you, regardless," Shamus said. "You are the kind of bewitching lady a man would protect and defend until his last breath."

"Silver-tongued devil," she muttered, though his words did make her heart dance with joy.

"I speak the truth." His gaze intensified on her. "I vow, I have never seen such a lovely lass as you are,

Lady Maili. 'Tis almost worth it, being in this filthy dungeon, just so I can enjoy your visits each day. You make it bearable. Otherwise, I would've already gone mad."

Her heart pounded at his words. Could she believe him?

"The only bad thing..." he said, "well, one of the bad things... is that I must smell like a beast, having been imprisoned here for days with no opportunity to bathe."

The whole dungeon smelled bad, so she had not noticed his scent. "I will have a servant bring you a bucket of water and soap," she said. "And clean clothes."

"I thank you." Shamus handed her the bottle through the bars.

She nodded, wishing she knew what to say to him. "I will send the servant." She rushed away, up the steps.

Secretly, Maili sent one of the kitchen servants to take Shamus a bucket of warm water, soap and a clean change of clothes. She didn't know why she hadn't thought of it earlier. Of course, he would wish to be clean, being a gentleman of his clan. She'd been far more concerned that he was fed and his wounds tended.

"Maili, I want to talk to you," her brother said in a stern voice as she crossed the great hall. Blast! Did he know of the bath and object to it? Had he heard from Shamus' brother?

"About what?" she asked.

"Come with me." Elrick led the way to his small meeting room down a short corridor off the great hall and closed the door behind them.

He turned to her and leaned against the door.

She felt trapped of a sudden. Was he blocking the door so she wouldn't try to flee the room?

"What is it?" she asked, though she was certain she wouldn't like his answer.

"I've arranged another betrothal for you."

"What? Nay. You ken I don't wish to marry." Why had her second sight not shown her this?

"I don't care what you want," Elrick said. "As is customary for the sister of a chief, your marriage will strengthen the clan."

"Who is the man?"

"Our guest, MacDonald of Sleat."

CHAPTER FIVE

"Are you mad?" Maili asked her brother, feeling as if a noose tightened around her neck. "I am too closely related to MacDonald of Sleat to marry him."

"Nonsense," Elrick said. "You're fourth cousins. The bard kens well both of your lineages."

Dear heavens, nay! Surely her brother could not be so malicious as to force her to marry Sleat. "He is an old man."

"Not that old." Elrick shrugged. "Merely two score and ten. And he is hale and hearty. A great warrior."

"Almost as old as Da." Regardless of his age, Sleat was not an attractive man. He always glared at everyone and belittled his men. He boasted in an annoying, loud voice at the high table. Not only that, she detested his lustful stares. Nausea rose within Maili. "That's why he has come here? Why did you not tell me earlier?"

"Nay, as I said, he came for clan business. When he saw you and observed you for a while, he decided to offer for you. Naught was decided until today."

"I won't marry him," she said firmly. "I refuse."

"You will do as I command. I wish Da hadn't spoiled you. You ken you must marry. Already, three men have rejected you because of how strange you are. Sleat is willing to overlook the rumors and your odd behavior. His first wife had the sight, so it is naught new to him. He has a fondness for witches."

"I am not a witch!"

Her brother smirked. "As well, he is willing to overlook your advanced age. At twenty-three summers, you are not likely to get any more offers of marriage."

She ground her teeth. She did not view herself as old or on the shelf. In fact, she still felt just as she had at eighteen. "When is this to take place?" she asked.

"Next week, after I exchange the prisoner for the ransom."

At noon the following day, Maili discretely gathered food in the kitchen for Shamus and wrapped it in a clean cloth. She feared if Elrick knew she was going to visit Shamus again, he might stop her, since he thought he was betrothing her to Sleat.

Only one week until she became the wife and thrall of that goat? Over her dead body!

She had hardly slept at all the night before as she tried to work out a solution in her mind. How could her brother be so vile as to arrange such a horrid marriage for her?

Now she knew why MacDonald of Sleat had been staring at her as if she were an oddity. He'd been trying to decide if she were truly mad or a witch he might tolerate as his wife. Bastard!

Well, she was having none of it. She would leave here with Shamus or die trying.

She slipped out the kitchen doorway and took a roundabout way to the dungeon entrance so that neither her brother nor any of Sleat's men saw her. The guard was not surprised to see her and barely gave her a nod before he let her pass.

When Maili's eyes adjusted to the dim torchlight of the dungeon, she couldn't believe how different Shamus looked. She hadn't even realized how dirty he'd been. His dark hair looked shiny and clean. Most of the swelling in his face had disappeared, too. 'Twas clear to her he was one of the best-looking men she had ever seen.

"I thank you for sending the bath," he said. "Feels much better to be clean."

She nodded and handed him the bread and cheese wrapped in a cloth. She couldn't tell him how much better he looked and how appealing she found him. She tried not to stare but found it difficult.

"You're quiet this day, Lady Maili," he murmured, studying her with dark, spellbinding eyes while he ate.

She shrugged and stared down at the bottle of ale in her hands so he wouldn't see how much she enjoyed looking at him. She was devastated at the thought she might be married to the MacDonald of Sleat chief within a week's time. If only Shamus were a free man who wished to marry her.

Mayhap she could help him to be a free man.

"May I have a sip of that?" he asked.

She nodded and removed the cork.

Taking the bottle she offered, he frowned. "Did your brother tell you not to talk to me anymore?"

"Nay. Of course not."

He drank a long swallow then moved closer to the bars. "What then?"

She took a wee step back, not because she feared him, but because his magnetic presence disturbed her and sent her heart racing with excitement and awareness. "'Tis naught."

"Look at me, Maili," he murmured.

When she did, his dark gaze in the torchlight penetrated into her very soul.

"Do you not ken 'tis dangerous to look at a man like that?"

He was teasing her again. She narrowed her eyes.

He grinned. "Come here." His words were soft but firm, like a gentle command. One she wanted to obey, but still she feared what would happen if he touched her. She knew not whether she could trust him. What if he grabbed her and choked her to death? Nay, he would not do such a thing, would he? Her second sight and her instincts told her he was far more trustworthy than her own brother.

Still, going near him made her nervous; she stood firm. "Why?"

"I want to ask you something." His voice was the epitome of seduction. Not that she had ever been seduced. But his tone affected her in startling ways that confused her.

"You can ask me from there." She placed her hands upon her hips.

"I ken it, but 'twould be much more enjoyable to whisper it into your ear."

The fear lingered. Would he grab her and hurt her? Or the opposite... grab her and kiss her? Either one was sure to change her world in unfathomable ways.

She had been betrothed thrice, but never kissed. Most men feared her; however Shamus didn't... because he had no knowledge of her gift. Once he learned of it, he might want naught to do with her again.

"You may tie my hands behind my back," he said.

His words startled her. "What? Why would I want to do that?"

"You don't yet trust me, do you?"

She shook her head, wishing she could trust him fully and completely.

"Well, if my hands are tied, you'll know I cannot touch you. You'll be safe. But you must untie me afterward."

She nodded, realizing this might be the way to get him to take her with him when he left. He seemed interested in her.

"I'm showing how much I trust you." He turned his back to her and held his hands together. Saints, how could he give her so much power? After tearing a strip from the cloth she'd bundled his food in, she tied his wrists together.

He faced her again, his lips quirking the slightest bit.

She lifted a brow. "Now, what do you wish to ask me?"

He moved his face next to the bars. "You're still not yet near enough for me to whisper in your ear."

She inched closer and turned her head, positioning her ear near his mouth. His breath teased her hair and her skin, giving her a shiver.

"Maili," he whispered, his warm lips brushing her ear.

Though she knew she should jump away and run, she could not. Instead, she wanted to lean into him, grab onto him. He smelled good—a clean male scent which was strange but alluring.

"May I kiss you?" he asked.

Breath refused to enter her lungs. 'Twas true, she'd

imagined what his lips might feel like on hers, dreamed about it. But to now be faced with the real possibility it could happen made her heart gallop within her chest.

"Will you allow me that great indulgence?" he persisted.

She wanted to protest and deny him. But her body would not cooperate with her mind. She tried to shake her head, but this only caused his lips to brush against her cheek. He kissed her there, emitting a soft breath.

"Kiss me, Maili," he urged.

She shook her head slightly. "I know not how," she whispered, heat and embarrassment burning over her.

"Come. I'll show you." His bewitching eyes were heavy-lidded in the dimness. "Press a kiss to my lips," he encouraged.

She cast a quick glance behind herself, toward the stairs, to make certain the guard hadn't sneaked into the dungeon. Then, turning back to Shamus, she gathered her courage and placed a brief kiss on his lips. The warm, sensual feel of them enthralled her and excitement swirled through her. She had finally done it—she had kissed a man.

When she drew back, he breathed, "Aye, that's it. Do it again."

Again? Saints, he was wicked. But since the first kiss had been so captivating, she wished to experience it again. When their mouths met this time, his tongue darted against her lips, shocking her, but she remained where she was, too intrigued to move.

"Sweet," he whispered. "Open your mouth. Let me taste you."

Although she did not understand why he would want to taste her, his words lured her, compelled her to do anything he asked.

Placing her hands upon his broad shoulders through the bars, she did as he asked and opened her mouth against his. Growling, he took possession, sliding his tongue inside. Soon, she understood what he was doing and flicked her tongue against his.

He groaned. "Aye, lass, you're a quick study. Again."

Unable to believe her own boldness, she darted her tongue into his mouth, then away, teasing him.

"Saints, you do try a man's patience." His eyes were heavily lidded as if he were half drugged on some unusual herb, and she could not resist his dark look of desire. Knowing she was walking a thin line of danger, she kissed him again, allowed him to kiss her in a way that made her feel she was barely a maiden anymore. He had turned her into a wanton. His tongue delved deeply into her mouth, making her wish he was out of that cell and pressing his hard body tightly to hers. She felt as if her insides were melting like warm honey.

"Saints, I want to hold you in my arms," he rasped, straining against the bars.

She stepped back, trying to regain control of herself. Every part of her felt on fire—her body, her heart, her soul. Never had another person awakened her spirit as he did. 'Twas almost as if she'd been half asleep until this moment.

"You must help me, Maili," he whispered. His fiery obsidian eyes pleaded with her.

"How?"

"Help me get out of here tonight."

Why would he ask this of her right after kissing her? "You're trying to manipulate me and use me?" Her heart ached with the realization.

"Nay. There is naught I like more than kissing you. But if I can get back home in time, my brother won't bring a fleet of galleys and attack your clan's castle. No one has to know you helped me."

"They will suspect." Aye, they would. But, regardless, she had to help him. 'Twas her only option if she wanted to avoid marrying Sleat. "If I help you escape, will you take me with you?" she whispered only louder than a breath.

Shamus watched her for a long moment, obviously thinking that over. "Much as I would like to, I cannot. Your brother would consider it abduction, even if you want to go. 'Twould cause clan war just as my imprisonment will."

She couldn't tell him that her brother had betrothed her to a chief, for it would make Shamus even more resistant to taking her with him. Bride thievery was a serious offense and would rile the two branches of the MacDonald clan.

"I must go," she said. She had to clear her mind and think.

"Wait, my hands are still tied."

"Very well. Turn around." When he did, she slipped the *sgian dubh* from the sheath on her ankle and cut the cloth binding his wrists. She had much to think over. If he wouldn't take her with him, did she truly want to help him escape only to get into trouble with her brother? He might beat her, or have one of his men do it. She started up the dungeon steps.

"I hope you'll return soon," Shamus called after her.

Aye, she would like to, but she didn't ken what to do. Exhausted as she was, she couldn't think clearly.

Had he only kissed her to sway her into helping him escape? Her heart sank. She had so hoped he might come to truly care for her.

She hurried across the courtyard and upstairs to her chamber, closed the door and barred it.

Her mind in turmoil, she paced until her heart rate and breathing calmed, then she built up the fire by adding dried peat. She could think of no other solution to all the problems than to assist him in escaping and then going with him, whether he wanted her to or not. She had to somehow convince him.

If she remained here, she would be married to Sleat in a week's time. Her life would be over. She simply could not imagine being married to the goat. He was old enough to be her father. Not only that, but he had a vicious look in his eyes. Hints of his cruelty leaked out here and there in the way he treated his men. He had grabbed her arse not one minute after he had entered Bearach Castle. He held no respect for women, whether they were ladies or not. Plus, if Shamus didn't get home before his brother brought a fleet of galleys and a huge garrison, most of her clan could be slaughtered.

Having slept little the night before because of worrying, Maili removed her *arisaid*, lay down on the bed and pulled the counterpane over her.

A few hours later, she awoke, gasping for breath. She had again seen the future and it was terrible.

The MacKenzie chief would attack their castle and lay waste to it. Most of the men would be killed. She saw the vision of their bloody bodies lying strewn about the bailey.

"Nay," she whispered, leaping to her feet. She had to do something. She had to figure out how to help Shamus escape so he could stop his brother.

But he'd said he couldn't take her with him if she did help him. She would go anyway, whether he liked it or not. She would follow.

A knock sounded at the door and she jumped.

CHAPTER SIX

Maili opened her bedchamber door to find one of the serving maids waiting there. "The chief sent me to fetch you to supper."

Maili now heard strains of music filtering up from the great hall. 'Twas the last place she wished to go. Her brother and Sleat were there.

"I have a headache. Please tell him I'm not feeling well and will sup in my room this eve."

"Very well, m'lady." The servant curtsied and left.

Maili closed the door. While belting her plaid *arisaid*, a quick plan formed in her mind. She then slipped down the back stairs, to the busy kitchen, where she wrapped two warm berry tarts in a cloth. The maids were so busy, they paid her little mind, except to curtsy in respect and rush to the next chore. She then took a loaf of bread and large chunk of cheese and wrapped them in another cloth. Three bottles of wine were the last items she snatched. She wrapped each in cloth so they wouldn't break, then crammed them into a satchel. She slipped out the kitchen portal and proceeded to the stables. Gloaming was nigh upon them and the torches in the bailey had been lit.

"Finnian, can you saddle my horse?" she asked the lanky thirteen-year-old stable lad. "I'm taking the healer into the village to visit a wee sick lad. If you promise to keep this a secret, I'll give you a treat."

Finnian's eyes widened. "What sort of treat, m'lady?"

"Two bramble tarts."

He grinned and raced to do her bidding, saddling Ruairi in only a few minutes. Her horse was a strong gelding who could handle two riders.

"You promise not to tell anyone I've gone?" she asked when Finnian had finished and stood before her expectantly.

"Aye, of course, m'lady. Upon my honor." He covered his heart with his hand and bowed.

"If anyone asks, tell them I must have saddled the horse myself. Hold Ruairi here. I'll be back for him in a few minutes. Here are your tarts." She handed him the cloth bundle. He'd already gobbled two bites by the time she left the stables.

Moments later, Maili huffed and gasped as she carried the large bucket of well water toward the entrance to the dungeon where the guard stood.

"Here, let me help you with that, Lady Maili."

"I thank you, Dugan."

He smiled and winked, then lifted the bucket as if it weighed naught. "You should not be carrying such a heavy load. Why did you not get one of the manservants to help you with it?"

"They're all busy with their chores."

"Where are you going with this?"

"I'm taking it to the prisoner. He has not bathed since he was brought in. He smells a fright." She already knew Dugan had not been on duty the night before, when the servant had brought the other bucket of water.

"Aye, naught worse than a stinking MacKenzie." He chuckled.

Wanting to stamp his toe, she ground her teeth and hid her displeasure. "Would you mind terribly carrying it down there for me? I must hurry, for supper will be starting soon."

"Nay, of course not. 'Twould be my pleasure to help you in any way I can." He turned to descend the dungeon steps.

She followed, wanting to kick herself because she'd forgotten to bring an empty wine bottle. She would simply have to use a full one. She slipped it from her satchel.

Please, God, forgive me. She lifted the bottle and smashed it against the back of Dugan's head. He went down like a crumbling stone wall. The scent of wine filled the air, and water from the bucket splashed everywhere. He made no sound, nor did he move.

She prayed she hadn't killed him, for he was the only guard who treated her kindly.

"Saints," Shamus hissed as he observed her through the bars.

"I'm sorry, Dugan," she whispered and pulled the ring of keys from his belt. With trembling hands, she fitted the key into the cell door lock and turned. A click sounded and she pulled the door open.

"Thank you, Maili." Shamus pulled her to him for a quick kiss on the lips which stunned her, but she had no time to enjoy the moment.

She knew Dugan carried a flask of whisky in his sporran at all times. She'd often seen him slip it out and take a sip. She removed it and poured it throughout the cell, to keep her brother's dog from being able to pick up Shamus' scent. He dragged

Dugan into the cell, divested him of everything but his long shirt, and put the plaid on himself over the plaid he already wore. "A disguise," he said, pulling the top portion of the plaid over his head. With cut strips of material, he tied Dugan's hands behind his back and put a gag into his mouth.

"I pray he lives," Maili said, locking him inside the cell. "But he will know I hit him. And report it to my brother."

"I doubt he will have any memory of it," Shamus said. "You must go back to your chamber, Maili, and act as if naught happened." Shamus secured Dugan's baldric, sword and dirk onto himself.

She chewed on her fingernail. "Take me with you," she whispered.

"Nay. I cannot. I told you. 'Twould be kidnapping."

She shook her head. "Not if I go willingly. Please. My brother will punish me severely for this. He will beat me."

"He will not know."

"Aye, he will. He kens well I have brought you many meals. The guard will awaken and remember that I bashed him on the head."

Giving her a dark look of regret, Shamus clenched his jaw. "I must go now before 'tis noticed the guard is gone." He proceeded up the steps toward the exit. She followed as quietly as she could but her breaths came in harsh gasps, not from exertion but from fear. She had to help Shamus escape these walls. This was best for him and her own clan, to protect them from his brother. But now she feared for her own life.

"I brought food," she said, walking briskly behind him toward the stables. Her gaze scanning the bailey, she saw no one about. Most were preparing for supper or serving the meal in the great hall.

"I thank you." Shamus slipped behind a post. "Where is it?"

"In a satchel, hidden in my *arisaid*. I'm coming with you."

"I told you nay, Maili. You will slow me down," he said in a fierce whisper.

She felt as if he'd knifed her in the heart.

"Do not look at me thus," he ordered in a quiet tone.

"I helped you. You're not willing to help me?"

"You'll be much safer here with your clan than you could ever be with me, on the run. I have no notion how I'll get back to my clan's lands. I have no galley. The land is rugged and the mountains high if I must go inland."

"I will keep up. I am strong." Tears burned her eyes.

"Maili," he beseeched her.

"You kissed me. I thought you cared."

"Of course, I care. 'Tis why I want you to stay where you'll be safe. If your brother gives chase, you could be injured."

She shook her head. "I know the area better than you. I know the best hiding places. I have a horse, and besides that, I have the keys to the postern gate."

"Give them to me."

"Nay."

The portcullis clanged, opening slowly.

Shamus moved behind the stable wall. Maili followed, covering her head with the plaid of her *arisaid*.

Three riders entered and dismounted before the

stables.

"See to our horses, lad," one of the men snapped at Finnian. All three hastened toward the great hall.

Finnian took one of the horses inside.

Shamus slipped forward and took the bridle of another.

Maili shook her head. "These horses are tired. My horse is rested and already saddled."

While Shamus hid behind the corner of the stables, Maili went inside and led out her large gelding.

Once she returned, she held out her hand to Shamus. "Here is the key for the postern gate. You go out that way and meet me between here and the village. Hide behind the bushes. I'll ride the horse through the gates and along the road."

Shamus nodded and headed away from her. She prayed he would not be seen and that the guards would not detain her.

Once she was perched upon Ruairi's back, she headed for the gates.

"I'm going to the village to visit a sick child," she told the two guards on duty. 'Twas naught unusual, for she had done this several times before, but she rarely rode out this late.

One nodded and they raised the portcullis. She tapped her heels against the horse's flank and he quickened his pace. Just before the village, she paused and glanced about the bushes. Where was Shamus?

"Shamus," she hissed.

Glancing behind, she discovered him, running to catch up to her. Breathing hard, he paused beside her, then leapt on behind. The horse startled, dancing about and snorting.

Stroking Ruairi's neck, she tried to soothe him.

"Shh, lad. 'Twill be all right."

"Let us be off before your brother discovers what's happened," Shamus murmured, his breath warming her ear.

Hiding her shiver of awareness, she guided the horse through the bushes and trees, around the edge of the village. She certainly didn't wish to have any witnesses to their escape.

Excitement raced through her veins, for she had avoided marrying Sleat, and she was on the run with a fine-looking warrior.

She did not know if Shamus would ever wish to marry her, but she'd try to convince him of her value as a wife. With him, she would always feel safe and cared for. She hadn't known him long but she knew he was a good man… and an expert at kissing.

"Your brother will be expecting us to travel north, toward MacKenzie territory," Shamus said, his warm breath sending delicious chills racing down her neck and across her breasts. "We need to head south and find a wee galley."

Amid the chaos of sensation storming through her, it took a moment for his words to register. Such a galley would be too small for her horse to board. She turned her head toward him. "I cannot leave Ruairi."

"Who?"

"My horse."

"'Twould be for the best, else your brother will accuse me of horse thievery along with kidnapping a lady. Do you wish me to hang?"

"Of course not! 'Tis my horse, a gift to me, personally, from my father. 'Tis not stealing if I take it myself."

"Very well. I'll have to think on it. Mayhap we can take a larger galley."

She nodded.

The longer they rode through the growing darkness, the closer Shamus sat against her. Or maybe she had slid back in the saddle, trying to absorb some of his warmth. She loved how protective he felt nestled tightly against her. Aye, that was it, though she wasn't truly afraid.

Regardless, his hard body rocking and stroking against her back bewitched her and near put her into a trance.

The wind picked up, blowing harder. He draped his plaid around them both, making her feel cozy and tingly. She wished they were lying before a warm fireplace on a sheepskin rug, snuggling naked beneath his plaid. What naughty things might he teach her?

Shamus wrapped his arms around Maili, holding the plaid in place and warming her in the windy darkness. He prayed a storm was not blowing in off the sea. Thus far, the sky was clear with only a cloud here and there.

He was glad for the excuse to hold her. 'Twas the first time he had done so, and though she was much smaller than his own tall frame, she fit perfectly in his arms. With the wind and their mad dash across the moor, the cowl of her *arisaid* had slipped off her head. He restrained the urge to kiss her ear and her neck. Surely the skin was as soft and smooth as velvet. He could not believe the excitement and arousal drumming through him.

He pressed his nose close to her hair. Her wondrous female scent stirred his desires, making him yearn to drag her back hard against his chest. She would feel so good lying upon him. A groan escaped him.

She turned her head. "Are you in pain?"

He choked back a laugh. "Nay." His voice sounded too rough to his own ears.

He hadn't meant to bring her with him. He could've said something scathing and harsh and she would've stayed back there. But he couldn't hurt her like that. Besides, her malicious brother might have punished her if he'd discovered she'd helped Shamus escape. He couldn't stand the thought of anyone hurting her. She was so small and delicate, like a fairy lass. Indeed, she stole his good sense away, causing him to want to do anything she wished.

The moon was high in the sky when tall silhouettes came into view on a hill in the distance.

"What is that?" Shamus whispered into her ear.

"*Clachan nan Sitheach.* The standing stone circle."

He had seen only one before in his life, a relic left over from the ancient past. Had it been built by their distant ancestors, or the fairies, as many believed?

A sudden shout echoed behind them, drifting on the harsh wind. A horse's neigh.

Dread surged through him. "God's teeth, they're not far behind us."

CHAPTER SEVEN

Hand on his sword hilt, Shamus turned to look back toward the shouting but saw nothing in the darkness. He couldn't believe her clan had noticed their absence so quickly.

Maili urged her horse to a faster pace. They raced toward the hill.

"I must hide you." Shamus was far more concerned for her safety than his own. "If they find you, tell them I kidnapped you and forced you to come with me."

"Nay, I will not." Sounding panicked, she drew up. "Come. Dismount." Maili slid off the horse. "We'll both hide."

Shamus followed suit. Though he would not normally hide from challengers, he was greatly outnumbered this time. "Where?"

"Among the standing stones and gorse bushes at the top of the hill. My clan won't go up there. They believe anyone who trespasses in the fairies' domain will be cursed."

"And you don't believe this?" he asked.

"Nay. I have been here before. If the fairies live here, they don't mind my visits." She led the horse up the hill into the circle. Shamus followed, spending half his time staring back toward the trail but seeing naught.

"You stay here and hide," he murmured. "I'll take the horse and ride on. They'll follow me and you can safely return to the castle." Though he did not want to leave her, 'twould be the best for her.

"Nay. I'll not have you accused of stealing a horse," she said in a fierce whisper.

"They'll not capture me," he assured her.

"Then why did we simply not ride on? I won't slow you down."

Damnation, Shamus could think of no ideal solution.

For a moment, all was silent save the wind and the horse chomping grass. Fortunately, the bushes here were tall enough to hide the horse.

"Will he stay quiet?" Shamus asked.

"Aye. I believe so."

Peering around a tall stone, Shamus watched as torches came into view around the bend. A dog's bark echoed through the night.

"Saints, they're tracking me with a dog," Shamus said, his stomach knotting.

"Don't fash. I doused the cell with whisky and you brought all your clothes with you."

"The dog could be tracking you."

"Oh, blast," she whispered. "I didn't think of that."

The dog might smell either of their scents, or even the horse's. Fortunately, they were downwind at the moment.

The dog and her clansmen swiftly passed by along the trail, the men sounding loud and unruly as if they were ready for battle. He could not see all of them by the light of a few torches, but suspected there were more than a dozen.

Soon, they were gone, moving inland.

"'Tis surprising the dog didn't smell us," Shamus said.

"This is a magical place, you ken." Maili sat on the ground and he joined her, sitting close enough for his arm to brush hers. How cozy this was, she thought, sitting here, sheltered from the wind and the eyes of her clan among the gorse bushes and standing stones with the most appealing man she'd ever met.

"Indeed?" he asked, skepticism and amusement clear in his voice. "Magical?"

"Of course. Do you not believe in things you cannot see or touch?"

"Aye, certainly." He paused for a moment. "I wonder... are you one of the fairies?"

"Ha. Nay, of course not." She eyed him through the darkness but could only see the outline of his form. Was he teasing or serious? 'Twas difficult to tell.

Her stomach growled.

"You sound hungry," he said.

"I am indeed. I haven't eaten since this morn."

'Haps Shamus was hungry, too. She dug into the pouch of her *arisaid,* pulled out the satchel and unwrapped the cloth. "Have some bread and cheese." She handed him chunks of the food.

"I thank you. I was hungry," he said between bites. Even then, his voice held a smooth, seductive quality. Or was she imagining things?

After eating a few bites, she uncorked the spiced wine she'd brought and sipped, then gave him the bottle.

The wine sloshed and he swallowed. "Delicious," he said, passing it back to her.

After corking the wine, she put it and the food away in her satchel.

"Is there another trail out of here?" he asked.

"Ben Clagen is to the north and Ben Milchen to the east. Both are high and craggy. We can cross neither. Even the pass is very high and rough. The best route is the way my clan went."

"'Tis too dangerous to follow them," he said. "They might turn back. Or hide and wait for us to approach."

"A few miles south, there is a fork in the trail. In the morn, we might be able to see their tracks and tell which way they've headed. 'Tis too dark now, even with the moonlight."

"Aye."

Because she was only able to discern his silhouette in the moonlight, the sound of his voice stirred up something strange but thrilling inside her.

What were they going to do for the rest of the night? Sleep? She was far too restless. Kiss? That thought sent a rush of heat through her. Was this desire she was feeling for the first time in her life? Was this the passion the bards and troubadours sang of?

Feeling disturbed and flushed, she arose and wandered to the central standing stone, the tallest. It had to be at least twelve feet in height. Legend said it was the marrying stone. She did not know whether to believe this or not... or even what it truly meant. She placed her hands flat upon it, as she had done a few times before. It had certainly never caused her to get married. In fact, all her suitors had been repelled.

Rocks clattered as Shamus approached. "'Tis a very tall stone." He tilted his head back to observe the top in the moonlight.

"Aye." She loved the smooth, weathered surface and the scratchy lichens growing on parts of it. When she closed her eyes, she felt the centuries these stones had stood witness to. They had existed here far longer than hundreds of years. 'Twas thousands of years they had stood just as they were now. With her "sight" she saw the ancient people who had come here. This had been a most sacred place to them. And then she saw the couples, hundreds of them, who had stood here touching the stone. It had bound them in a love so strong, none had ever parted. Even though death had separated some of them briefly, they had remained soul mates, and rejoined in the afterlife. Tears pricked her eyes at the depth of emotion and love. This was the kind of love she wanted.

"Maili, are you all right?" Shamus asked in a gentle voice.

She opened her eyes to find him leaning against the stone.

"Why are you crying?"

She shook her head, her throat too tight to speak. She could never explain what she saw. It was too grand, too elaborate and complicated. Infinite love.

He pushed away from the stone and drew nearer. With his thumbs, he stroked her tears away, then leaned in and kissed her. Keeping one hand on the stone, she placed the other around his waist. How profoundly his kiss affected her. She felt as if that same powerful emotion she'd sensed coming from the couples thousands of years ago, who'd joined here, was surging through her. Love and need so strong she could hardly breathe.

Her heart pounded and she pulled him tighter

against her, kissing him with more fervor. His heart beat hard against her breast.

She grew frantic at the overwhelming intensity of emotion. "Shamus," she gasped between kisses.

"Aye, Maili." He sounded as profoundly affected as she was, and his kisses grew more insistent, more ardent.

Good heavens! Had the stones joined them?

Shamus drew Maili tight against him and took possession of her sweet mouth again. He flicked his tongue between her lips. Saints, but she was passionate and delectable. He wanted to devour her on the spot.

Her hands tangled in the hair at the nape of his neck and before he knew what he was about, he had her lying on the grass-softened ground. He drew back and lay beside her so as to not frighten her.

But she did not seem afraid. In fact, she grasped the top of his plaid and pulled him down to her again. The kiss resumed, slower and more sensuous this time. 'Slud! Either she was a quick study or she'd lied about not knowing how to kiss. Was she more experienced than she admitted? He didn't care. He simply wanted her.

Wishing her to know how powerfully she affected him, he pressed his hard shaft against her hip.

A startling feeling ricocheted through him—the realization that he would do anything to protect her. That she belonged beside him. His instincts urged him to yank up her skirts and take her, make her his mate, his wife.

Damnation, he couldn't do that.

Grinding his teeth, he pulled her hands from around his neck and shoved to his feet.

"We must stop now, Lady Maili," he growled, turning away from her. He tried to calm his breathing and the excitement rampaging through him. Saints, how he desired her. He had never felt such intensity before.

"Why must we?" she asked in a small voice.

He turned to glare at her through the moonlight. He could barely discern the outline of her form where she sat on the ground by the tall stone. "You don't ken?" he demanded. Did she not feel the need as he did?

"Well... I was enjoying it," she confessed.

He let out a humorless laugh. In his view, that was putting it mildly. He reveled in her. He could devour her, lose himself in her.

"Did you not?" she asked in a puzzled voice.

"Aye, lass, I was enjoying it far too much, if you grasp my meaning."

She remained silent.

"You don't have an inkling what I'm talking about, do you?" he asked, keeping his voice low.

"Not... fully. I didn't ken it was possible to enjoy something *too* much."

He blew out an exasperated breath. How could she be so guileless and innocent? "Is it true you had never been kissed before I kissed you in the dungeon?"

"Of course. I would not lie," she said, her tone quiet but defensive.

She was so naïve, 'haps she was younger than he'd imagined. "How old are you?"

"Three and twenty," she snapped, rising to her

feet. "You think simply because of my advanced age I should've been kissed long ago. I ken it. I was betrothed three times." Her voice caught with emotion.

A shock went through him. "Nay, I thought you younger. Pray pardon. I didn't mean to upset you." Saints! The last thing he wanted to do was make her cry.

"'Tis naught," she whispered, turning away. The tears in her voice flayed him.

"Three and twenty is young. I'm five years older." He feared his lame attempt at soothing her wouldn't work, but he wished to know more about her. "What happened... with the betrothals? Why did you not marry?"

"None of them would have me after they... heard the rumors." Her voice hitched.

"What rumors?"

She shook her head. "I would rather not say."

Nay, she wouldn't have him believe her a witch like everyone else did. She wanted Shamus to like her, to take her with him to his clan's castle. He was an honorable man who would protect her. Not like the cowards who accused her of witchcraft.

"You can trust me. I'll not judge you."

His smooth, rich voice sounded soothing in the darkness, and somehow she believed him. Still, she didn't wish him to know. 'Twould change things. He might even leave her here, if he feared witches.

"Very well, then," he muttered. "Don't trust me."

She turned halfway. "I do... trust you, but 'tis difficult for me to talk about it. I hope you can understand."

Her horse started down the other side of the hill.

"Where's he going?" Shamus asked.

"Mayhap he's thirsty and kens there's a small loch at the bottom of the hill."

Thankful for the excuse to escape the conversation, she caught up with Ruairi, led him down the hill to the water's edge, then held his bridle while he drank. Moonlight and the tall mountains around them reflected off the dark water.

"Is it deep?" Shamus asked from a few yards away.

"Toward the center it is. But the edges are shallow. I have swum here before."

"You have?" His voice held surprise. "Nude?"

"Nay! I wore a smock."

She could not believe her eyes when Shamus started disrobing. "What are you about?" she asked.

"I'm needing a wee swim. The cold water will... feel good. At home, I swim often in one of the three lochs that converge at Teasairg."

Although she knew she should not watch him in the faint light, she could not look away. When he tossed down his last garment—his shirt—and stood naked, she could not believe how the moonlight glanced off his broad shoulders and the muscles of his arms and legs. Before she could discern any more detail, he waded into the loch and took off swimming.

Ruairi lifted his head, water dripping from his mouth, and perked his ears at Shamus.

"He is mad, is he not?" she whispered.

Shamus swam back and forth across the center of the small loch twice. Heavens, he had endurance, and she was glad to see his shoulder was well recovered. Obviously, he was a tough Highlander. She had a wild urge to jump in herself, but she was not such a strong swimmer.

He ducked beneath the water in the center of the

loch and all went still. Where had he gone? Was he well? She scarce dared to breathe.

With a splash, he broke the surface close in front of her, startling both her and Ruairi. The horse jerked his head and snorted.

"Blast you," she muttered and tried to breathe normally again.

He chuckled, then strode onto shore where he'd left his clothes a few yards away. He flung back his hair and observed her for a long moment in the dimness. The intimate areas of his body were in shadow, but the silhouette of his lean muscular form, his broad shoulders, trim hips, and strong thighs, did strange things to her. Made her feel warm and tingly inside.

Slowly, silently, he moved toward her. What was he about?

CHAPTER EIGHT

Shamus placed his wet hand against Maili's jaw and neck, drawing her to him. Shivers raced over her. He kissed her long and deep, with such passion she grew lightheaded. Though the rest of him was cool, his mouth was hot. She held onto his wet, slick skin, but her knees grew weak as her instincts urged her to submit to him. Give him what he craved, for 'twas the same thing she craved.

The strong feeling that he was her man, her husband, and her soul mate burst through her.

"Shamus."

When he released her and drew away, she wanted to protest. But after grabbing his clothes, he lifted her into his arms and carried her up the hill. Among the standing stones, he lay her down on a soft, sheltered, grassy spot between the bushes.

"I want you, Maili," he whispered in a desperate tone, placing kisses down her neck. "I don't ken why but..."

"Aye," she urged. *You are mine, Shamus.* She wanted to tell him, but feared her words might cause him to stop.

"I don't wish to hurt you," he said, unbuckling the belt of her *arisaid*.

She shook her head. "You won't."

Oh, aye, she wanted out of her clothing. She wanted to feel his bare skin against hers. The wind had calmed here among the stones and her skin felt as if it were burning.

He tugged the clothing from her body and laid her upon his plaid. The water had dried from his skin and it felt warm and seductive sliding against hers. His hair was still wet and droplets from it cooled her face.

He kissed her, drugging her as a love potion might. His stone hard shaft pressed against her thigh. She had never felt anything so arousing. She shifted, turning toward him so she could feel his hard length pressing against her lower belly. She gave in to the urge and thrust her hips against his, yearning for him with a breathless ache.

"Och! Maili." He spread her thighs and settled between, then pulled her knee up beside his hip. He kissed her again, slow and deep. All the while the ache for him intensified. He moved down and brushed his warm lips over her breast, then drew the hard tip into his mouth. Good heavens, she had never felt anything so enticing. Combing her fingers through his damp hair and holding his head, she arched her body to him, offering him more. She became desperate and frantic with need.

When the tip of his erection touched her in that most intimate spot, a shock went through her. She gasped. Though she feared that large, male part of him would hurt her, she craved it with such intensity she thought she would go mad.

"Please," she breathed.

"Maili, love, you are the sweetest, most delicious..." He kissed her and stroked himself against her. She was surprised at the hot, slick moisture she felt between them. Saints, but he was making her burn and ache. She widened her thighs, hoping he would hurry and ease whatever mad fever he had afflicted her with.

With a sudden thrust, he was inside her. The pain of it shocked her and she cried out, tears pricking her eyes. Heavens! Had he caused her serious injury?

"Shh, lass, the pain will be over in a moment." He held still, kissing her face, stroking her body. He moved down and trailed his tongue over her nipple, then drew it into his mouth.

"Aye," she whispered. The more he suckled, the more her body heated and the more she grew accustomed to his invasion of her body. Her inner muscles clenched, caressing him.

He growled and moved a bit, a slight withdrawal. But nay, she did not want him to leave her. She thrust her hips.

"Oh saints, Maili," he hissed and pressed himself deeper still. The sharp pain returned and she dug her nails into his back.

"Shh. Remain calm, *mo graibh*." Gently he withdrew and inched back in.

'Twas not so bad that time. The next time was even better. As he slowly, gently moved, her body relaxed and she began meeting each of his thrusts, which gained speed and force. Such bliss he showered upon her.

He growled Gaelic words in her ear about how amazing she felt, along with endearments, but she could scarce pay attention to them. She'd had no idea lovemaking was like this—a delightful and pleasurable paradise.

As he moved, he lifted his upper body and

propped on his hands, then gazed down at her. She could not see his eyes as she wished to, for they were in shadow. But as she observed his long dark hair, his broad shoulders, and the side of his square jaw, hard with passion, a mysterious sensation swelled within her, like a whirlpool of tingles spiraling through her body, taking her down into pure bliss and then it shattered within her, like thousands of stars exploding.

He moaned and shoved into her, where he held himself, his body shuddering. "Aye, Maili, you are mine," he growled.

After a moment, he rolled to the side, breathing hard, and pulled her close to him.

Tears of gratitude and love dripped from her eyes. She didn't know how it was possible she could love him so soon. But she did. The marrying stone must have somehow forged a soul-deep bond between them. She knew he had to feel it, too, given what he'd just said to her.

"And you are mine, Shamus," she whispered, touching his scratchy, beard-roughened cheek. The words could have been marriage vows, considering how committed to him she felt.

His breathing calming, he kissed her forehead, then tugged the plaid over them into a warm cocoon.

⁂

What the devil had just happened? Shamus couldn't figure it out. He had bedded lasses before, but never had it been like this. Not wanting to let Maili go, he tightened his arms around her. He knew not what to say to her after that. He was near speechless. Baffled. Pulling her snug against his chest soothed him and made him relax. Her gentle hands moved over his bare back, stroking and caressing him. His heart pounded hard when he realized how precious she was to him. Och! He did not understand it. Never had he felt this way about a lass after lying with her, nor ever, for that matter.

With the warm, woolen plaid over them and her safely tucked into his arms, he grew groggy. The next thing he was aware of was opening his eyes to early dawn light and cool white mist trailing through the stones around them. The mist moved as if it contained a life of its own. Fingers of pink dawn light slid through.

"'Tis beautiful," he breathed.

Maili awoke and her eyes widened upon him, as if shocked to remember what they'd shared... and that they were still naked beneath the plaid.

"Look." He nodded toward the colorful sunrise beaming through the mist among the tall stones.

She turned her head. "Oh," she breathed in wonder. "How lovely."

"Aye." But he only had eyes for her now. "And you are lovely." With her head still turned aside, he kissed her ear, her throat. Her arms wound around his neck and she shivered. He moved down, placing wee cherishing kisses on her chest. When he reached her breast, he drew the rigid tip into his mouth. "Mmm," he breathed. Arousal surged through him, and he pushed his hardened shaft against her thigh.

"Shamus," she whispered.

"Aye." He shifted his attention to her other nipple, kissing and suckling.

"I hate to say this," she said, "but I must... excuse

myself."

With regret, he lifted his head. "Of course. Me too. We need to be on our way soon, anyway." Unfortunately.

He wished he could stay here with her forever.

But a threat lingered about them. Once they discerned which way the MacDonalds had gone, they would head along the alternate route out of the area.

Naked, he helped her dress in the pink dawn light. He then pulled his shirt over his head, belted his plaid about his waist and donned the baldric and weapons. She moved into the bushes and short trees out to the side of the stone circle.

"Don't go far," he warned, then realized it had been a while since he'd seen her horse. After he relieved himself, he glanced about for Ruairi but saw naught. He shook his head, trying to clear it. While within the stone circle, he'd felt drugged and blissful. A pleasant experience to be sure with Maili, but now, reality returned with a vengeance. Her brother's men were out scouring the countryside for them.

When Maili returned from the bushes, he said, "We must find your horse. I wonder if he's still by the loch."

"Oh." Her eyes widened and she glanced about. "I'd forgotten about him because of…" Her gaze flew to him and a lovely blush brightened her cheeks.

"Aye." He understood her meaning perfectly. "As did I. Come." He helped her down the hillside to the loch's edge. Pink dawn light reflected in the water's still surface and white mist floated above it.

The horse was nowhere to be seen in either direction. He muttered a curse beneath his breath. He should've led the horse back to the stone circle with them last night and tethered him to a bush. But Maili, and the passion between them, had so distracted him, a horse was the last thing on his mind.

"Do you think he returned to Bearach Castle?" he asked.

"Mayhap. He does love oats for breakfast."

'Slud. What would her clan think when the horse returned without her? Likely 'twould cause them to redouble their efforts in locating her. "We must continue our travels on foot, then."

Once on the muddy trail her clansmen had taken the night before, he paused often, listening for any sounds that might tell him the men were returning.

Two hours later, at the fork in the trail, he discovered fresh tracks going in both directions.

"Damnation," he muttered. "The search party split here. Which route offers ample hiding places and bushes along it?" he asked her.

Maili considered for a moment. "The trail south, I'm thinking."

He nodded, preferring to travel south along the coast anyway, where he might find a galley to transport them north again to his clan's castle.

After they'd each eaten a bannock while taking cover in a small wood beside the trail, he held her hand as they strode briskly along the narrow path, worn down from years of horse and foot traffic.

A horse snorted off to the left of the trail, in the bushes. Shamus drew his sword. Was that Ruairi or a different horse? He dragged Maili for cover in the bush on the opposite side of the path but before they were out of sight, a horse and rider burst onto the trail.

"Halt!" the bearded man yelled, his sword pointed

at Shamus. Three armed men on foot stood at the ready beside him.

'Twas the MacDonalds, of course. The bastard on horseback was the chief's war leader.

"Go, hide in the bushes," he told Maili.

Instead, she leapt in front of him. "Do not hurt him, Hamish!"

Shamus pushed her behind him but she wouldn't stay put. She moved around his other side, flattened herself against his chest and wrapped her arms tightly around him.

"Maili," he grumbled. How did she expect him to fight like this?

"Step aside, m'lady," Hamish ordered. "I'll not kill this kidnapping bastard until your brother gives me leave to do so, but I might teach him a lesson or two." He sent Shamus a malicious grin.

He would love to fight this whoreson, one on one. But this clan wouldn't give him that opportunity. He was constantly outnumbered. In fact, three more MacDonalds materialized out of the bushes. Seven to one.

"Nay!" Maili shouted. "You will not touch him! He didn't kidnap me. I left of my own free will."

"I didn't ken your brother allowed you to make such decisions." Hamish smirked. "But you can take that up with him."

"I shall."

"Disarm him and tie him up," Hamish commanded the other clansmen.

They rushed to do his bidding. Shamus had little choice but to give up his weapons without a fight. He did not want Maili hurt in the ruckus. And she refused to turn him loose.

"Step aside, m'lady," Hamish ordered in a more forceful tone.

"Do not hurt him or you will regret it!"

One of her clansmen pried her arms from around him, picked her up and carried her away.

"Leave her be!" Shamus growled.

"You're not the one giving orders, you whoreson!" Hamish said.

The man set Maili on her feet some distance away. When she tried to escape, he held her in place.

The men yanked at his arms, causing his shoulder —which had been healing—to twist painfully as they tied his hands behind his back. He grimaced but refused to allow them to know of the pain.

"When your horse returned to the castle afore dawn, we kenned you were close by," Hamish said with a smug grin. "'Twas only a matter of finding you."

Damnation, he'd known the horse would give them away.

One of her clansmen led Ruairi from the bushes.

"Mount so we can be on our way," Hamish told her.

When she hesitated, the man restraining her lifted her into the saddle.

"Master MacKenzie will ride with me," she announced.

Shamus was proud of her boldness and bravery but he feared it would get her into trouble, especially where her brother was concerned. In fact, he feared her brother might punish her for helping Shamus escape. He cursed under his breath. How could he have let this go so wrong?

"Nay, MacKenzie will be walking," Hamish said.

"Then I will, too." She dismounted.

Hamish released what sounded to be an exasperated breath. "Suit yourself, m'lady. But you must keep up."

Shamus considered various methods of escape on the way back to the castle, but he knew none of them would work. Not with Maili so close by. He would do naught to cause her injury. Now and then, he glanced at her, walking beside him. Every time her blue eyes met his, he could not fathom why his heart pounded and excitement raced through him. What magical powers did she hold over him? Did it have something to do with the standing stone circle? And the most difficult question of all—how could he escape the MacDonald clan and make her his wife?

CHAPTER NINE

Once they reached the castle, Elrick awaited them in the bailey and a frisson of fear raced through Maili. His glare darted between her and Shamus. Sleat stood nearby, scowling. Elrick strode toward them and threw a hard punch into Shamus' stomach.

"Stop!" She launched herself at her brother, but the large guard behind her caught her around the waist, her arms and legs flailing.

"You bastard!" Elrick said to Shamus. "How dare you kidnap my sister?"

Shamus was doubled over, gasping for breath.

"Leave him be!" Maili shouted. "He didn't kidnap me. I left because I wanted to."

"Take her upstairs and lock her in her bedchamber," he ordered the man restraining her.

The giant picked her up, threw her over his shoulder and carried her up the steps.

"Nay! You bastard! Release me!" She kicked and punched. Once inside the stairwell, he slapped her hard on the arse.

She screamed. "How dare you? Beast!"

He merely laughed. "Want me to do it again?"

Suddenly, defeat pressed in on her and tears streamed from her eyes. She couldn't best this hulking guard. He was solid muscle and weighed near thrice as much as she did. Once he'd opened her bedchamber door, he carried her inside and tossed her onto the bed.

Though she felt dizzy, she rolled toward the opposite side.

Once her vision focused, she saw that he leered at her with lascivious interest. She couldn't remember his name, but she knew he was one of the new guards Elrick had hired.

"What is going on, Maili?" Constance rushed forward. "Where have you been?"

The guard cast a glower at her cousin, then trailed his lustful gaze over Maili again. Thank the saints her cousin was here. Though they were not close, Maili ran toward her and embraced her.

"You can go now," she told the guard.

He lifted a brow as if to say this wasn't finished. Once he'd exited, she barred the door from the inside.

"Did the MacKenzie prisoner kidnap you when he escaped?" her cousin asked.

Maili paced before the warm hearth. "I don't wish to speak of it now."

Constance fell silent but Maili felt her gaze burning into her. "You helped him escape, did you not? You've been taking him food all week. Did he seduce you?"

Maili stopped and glared. How could her cousin guess such things? "Nay!"

Constance crossed her arms over her chest and cast a scornful look at Maili. "I don't believe you."

"I want to be alone." Maili needed to think, plan her next course of action. Her brother would no doubt toss Shamus in the dungeon again, if he didn't kill him. *Please, God, nay.* Surely he wouldn't because he needed him alive in order to exchange him for the ransom.

"Very well. But you are daft to help such an outlaw and scoundrel."

"He is neither an outlaw nor a scoundrel!" Maili said.

Her cousin removed the bar from the door and yanked at it, but it wouldn't budge.

Maili felt sick. "Elrick had the guard lock me in."

"But not me. I'm no traitor." Constance banged on the door. "Let me out of here!"

Maili was no traitor either, at least not to her clan. Helping an innocent man escape didn't mean she'd betrayed her clan. She was trying to help them avoid attack. As for Elrick, she was no longer loyal to him.

Several minutes later, a key rattled in the lock and the door opened. As her cousin left, her maid entered. And the guard outside quickly locked the door again. Thankfully, he was not the same one who had carried her in.

"M'lady!" Anora rushed forward and grasped her hands. "Are you well? What happened?"

"Aye, I'm fine. Don't fash. What is happening outside?"

"The chief had the guards take MacKenzie to the dungeon."

"Did they beat him?"

Her maid swallowed hard. "I fear they did."

The nausea churning through her increased. "That bastard," she said through clenched teeth. Was it a sin to hate one's own brother so? He was a vile, heartless man. She paced from the window to the door and back again. She could not abide it. She had to find a way to get to Shamus, to help him, to be with him.

Her thoughts were a jumble and she could not think of a plan.

Moments later, the key rattled in the lock. Mayhap she could run past the guard and escape, or bash him on the head. Frantically, she scanned the room for a weapon and her gaze landed on a stoneware jug.

As she ran toward it, the bedchamber door slammed back against the wall. Elrick stood there, his broad shoulders blocking the doorway. Too late to surprise him with a jar to the head, she halted.

"Out!" he yelled to Anora.

Tears in her wide eyes, the young maid fled the room, and Elrick slammed the door behind her.

"How could you betray me and the clan in such a way?" Elrick demanded. "I should deal with you as I would any traitor." He lurched forward and she ducked back, but not in time to avoid his fist flying toward her face. The blow to the jaw knocked her to the floor. Pain lanced through her face and shoulder which had struck the wood floor.

"I cannot wait until you are gone from here with Sleat!" he growled. "I never want to lay eyes on you again, witch."

Her throat closed on the shock and pain. Tears burned her eyes, more from the emotional pain than the physical, although both were severe. Elrick had never struck her before. Their father would've broken his nose if he had. She inhaled deeply, trying to regain her bearings. *Remain calm.*

She hoped if she didn't respond to him or talk back, he would leave her be.

"What do you have to say for yourself?" Standing over her, he crossed his arms over his chest.

What a self-important bastard her brother was. "If

Father were here he would—"

"Well, he isn't here to spoil you anymore, Maili! 'Tis time to grow up."

She ground her teeth and sat up, her hand covering her aching jaw. She worked it to make sure it wasn't broken.

"Dugan told me you hit him on the head with a bottle and knocked him out. How did MacKenzie convince you to help him?"

Maili pushed slowly to her feet, trying to hide her pain from her demented brother, and eased toward the other side of the room. "I was trying to protect our clan. I thought if he wasn't here, his older brother wouldn't lay siege." 'Twas the truth, at least half of it. She couldn't tell her brother the other half—that she wanted to escape this place, and him. Of course, he could probably figure that part out on his own.

"Ha," Elrick scoffed. "I'm not concerned about his brother. He may attempt an attack but he and his men will be shot down with flaming arrows. I have men about everywhere, on the lookout for MacKenzies."

She wanted to ask if he'd hurt Shamus, but she knew her concern would only make matters worse. She prayed his injuries weren't too severe.

"Did the bastard seduce you?" Elrick narrowed his eyes.

"Nay." Her answer was perhaps too quick, but she didn't view what she and Shamus had shared as his seducing her. Maybe she had seduced him. Or maybe the stones had brought them together in a spiritual and physical bond.

"You have lain with him," Elrick growled. "I can tell by the look in your eyes."

She dropped her gaze to stare at the floor. People had told her that her emotions were always plain to see.

"Not a word about it to Sleat! Do you hear me? You will trick him into thinking you're a virgin."

She frowned, wondering how she was supposed to do that. She knew little about coupling as it was. Not that she would marry Sleat, anyway. As soon as she could, she would escape this place, even if she had to hire a galley to take her to the small island where they suspected her brother Neacal was. He was not as cruel as Elrick. In fact, she was certain he would be on her side.

"You will marry Sleat as soon as the priest arrives, whether that be one day or five," Elrick said.

Saints, she had to devise a way out of this room.

"Prepare for your wedding and forget the MacKenzie outlaw. You will never see him again." Elrick walked out and slammed the door behind him. A second later the lock clicked.

Late that night, Maili dreamed, terrifying images running through her head. The MacKenzie chief was coming. She saw him, a tall, dark and fearsome warrior, disembarking from his clan's large fleet of galleys. What seemed like hundreds of soldiers armed with swords, battleaxes, dirks, targes and other weapons raced along the shore toward their castle. Bearach's walls were thick and strong. Surely no one could breach them. But then she heard the battle cries and saw the combat raging in the bailey.

"Nay!" She lurched upright in her bed, darkness

surrounding her. Cold sweat drenched her body.

"What is it?" Anora asked from her pallet near the hearth.

"I had a nightmare." Maili tried to calm her breathing, but the icy terror would not leave her. She shoved out of bed and crept to the window. Were the MacKenzies coming? No moon was visible. Thick clouds cast the night in blackness. Even if they were approaching, she could not see them.

Although her brother and some of his soldiers treated her poorly, most of her clansmen were good people. She didn't wish to see any of them hurt or killed because of Elrick's cruelty.

Staring out into the darkness, she thought she saw a movement on shore. She gasped, but saw naught more.

Nay, 'haps her eyes were playing tricks on her.

"M'lady, you're scaring me," her maid said.

"Aye, well. I'm scared."

"Why?"

A flaming arrow blazed through the darkness. In the far distance, a man cried out.

"Oh dear heavens, it has started! God help us all."

"What has started?" Anora raced toward her.

"The siege. The MacKenzies have come for their brother. Pray that not too many of our clansmen are killed."

More fiery arrows were shot in both directions. Distant shouts and metal clangs from the clashing of swords echoed from the opposite side of the castle.

"Oh, m'lady," her maid sobbed. "Do you think they will kill us?"

Shamus awoke with a start. A noise had sliced the silent darkness of the dungeon. When he moved to get up, pain lacerated his body. He groaned. The bastards had beaten him black and blue again. Not his face this time, but his body. No doubt so he wouldn't look so terrible when his brother came with the ransom money. He didn't think any of his bones were broken but he would surely have bruises over most of his body.

The sound reached him again—the clash of swords. He held his breath, listening. Aye, men shouting in the distance, at ground level.

Had Cyrus launched an attack? Grinding his teeth, Shamus pushed to his feet and limped toward the locked cell door. Breathing hard against the excruciating pain, he held onto the iron bars. Once the pain lessened a wee bit, he tried to breathe normally and listen.

Shouts echoed.

Where was Maili? He prayed she was safe in her chamber, away from the skirmish. He wished he could tell her to bar her door. Not that Cyrus or any of his brothers would harm her. But who knew about the hired guards and other soldiers?

Sword clangs at the top of the dungeon steps tensed his muscles. His brothers must have come!

A man cried out in a rough shout, then all grew quiet. Who had been killed? He prayed it wasn't one of his brothers, dead for attempting to rescue him.

Keys jangled.

Footsteps pounded down the stone stairs into the dungeon. A fast approaching torch blinded him.

"Shamus? Thanks be to God, you're alive!" his

second oldest brother said.

"Aye, Dermott!" Shamus grinned, despite the pain. "'Tis about time you got your arse here."

His brother shoved a key into the lock and turned. "We came as soon as we got the message you were taken hostage. Before that, we thought you'd drowned in the storm. Are you injured?"

"A few bruises and scrapes." Once the cell door was open, Shamus emerged. "What of Fraser?"

"He's outside, fighting beside Cyrus. We found him and the other men from your wrecked galley the next morn, but we couldn't find you. Have they been feeding you?"

"Aye, the chief has a sister who brought me food."

"Ah... a sister?" Dermott said in a teasing tone.

"Aye, we must take her with us when we leave this hell-pit."

"You mean to steal yourself a bride?"

Imagining Maili as his bride, Shamus held back a grin. "You could call it that."

"Saints!"

Shamus limped toward the stairs and sharp pains gored him. He hunched forward, a groan escaping him before he could prevent it.

"What did they do to you?"

Shamus stopped, breathing hard and praying the pain would vanish. "To make a long story short, the lady helped me escape last night, but we were caught this morn. Her brother and his men gave me a sound thrashing for it."

"Bastards," Dermott ground out. "You'll stay by my side."

Shamus dragged himself up the steps after his brother. At the top, next to the guard's dead body,

Dermott paused, snatched the man's sword and turned to Shamus. "Are you able to wield a blade?"

"Aye." His sword arm was still in fairly good shape.

Dermott handed him the guard's sword, dirk and targe. "Remember to stay behind me."

"Aye, we must retrieve Maili from her chamber. Her brother will punish her severely for helping me if she remains here."

Once they reached the bailey, Shamus frowned at all the men lying unmoving in the torchlight. Were they MacKenzies or MacDonalds? Upon further inspection, he saw that all of them except one were MacDonalds.

"Shamus!" His oldest brother approached, his clothing and face splattered with blood. "Glad I am to see you alive and kicking." Cyrus grabbed him around the neck.

Pain shot through his body and he growled before he could stop himself.

"What is it?" Cyrus released him, scrutinizing him through the dimness. "Are you hurt?"

"They beat him," Dermott said.

Shamus breathed sharply, willing the pain away. Damnation, the side of his chest hurt. He might have a broken rib.

"How badly?" Cyrus asked. "Do you have any broken bones?"

"I'm not certain. 'Haps a cracked rib." Shamus clenched his teeth, trying to downplay his injuries. Real men didn't whimper and moan.

"Bastards," Cyrus growled. "I'll give them what they're asking for."

Fraser approached but Shamus barely had time to

greet his younger brother before more MacDonalds rushed from the castle's portal.

"Kill them all!" Elrick yelled, his voice echoing between the castle's high walls.

"Their chief," Shamus told his brothers.

"He's the one I want, then," Cyrus said. "Stay between us."

The four brothers advanced toward Elrick and his five bodyguards. Shamus struck out at the one closest to him, but he lifted his targe to block the blow. Much swordplay ensued and after a few more slices, Shamus cut the man's throat.

When his foe dropped to the cobblestones, Shamus lifted his gaze to Elrick. The fighting continued around him, but his sights were set on the whoreson who had beaten him while his hands were tied. A spark of fear widened Elrick's eyes for an instant. Shamus sent him a humorless smile and rushed him.

His pain and injuries forgotten in the bloodlust quickening his body, Shamus slashed at the whoreson, from the right and the left, driving him backward, his sword cutting chunks from the other man's wooden targe.

The tip of Elrick's blade cut Shamus' arm but 'twas shallow and he barely felt the burn. He slipped a sword thrust beneath the other man's targe. His weapon drove deep into Elrick's abdomen.

Elrick shouted and dropped, then kicked about upon the ground, groaning and crying out.

From the corner of his eye, Shamus glimpsed another man charging him. Before he could turn and raise his targe, a blade cut deep into his upper arm—his sword arm. Though he tried, he could not raise his sword. The next slice was to his abdomen. Pain pierced through him. With his targe, he blocked the next blow but could not strike out and defend himself.

Cyrus dragged his attacker off. The two struggled, trying to dirk each other.

Shamus glanced down, seeing his sleeve and his shirt drenched in blood. He even felt the liquid heat of his blood soaking down into his plaid. Without the use of his sword arm, he was as good as dead if someone came at him. Although he could still use the dirk he grasped in his left hand.

He glanced about, aware he couldn't think clearly, then noticed everything fading to darkness. He tried to stay on his feet but the night closed in on him. He toppled to the cobblestone ground.

CHAPTER TEN

Maili stood at her chamber door, listening in the darkness. The sword clangs were fewer and farther between now, and she thought she heard women's sobs.

Dear God in Heaven, please don't let all the MacDonald men be dead. And Shamus... most of all, please keep him safe.

Her stomach ached. What was happening out there?

She banged on the door as she had countless times already. "Unlock this door!" She needed her freedom so she could see if Shamus was all right.

No one responded. Her guard must have gone outside to join in the fighting.

Her maid cowered in the corner, praying and crying.

Finally, the key wiggled in the lock and a click sounded. Who was releasing her? She had left the candles unlit so she might see out the window more easily.

She stepped back, then froze. The door creaked open slowly and a man stood on the threshold. The candle in his hand cast odd shadows upon his bearded face. Sleat? What in blazes was he doing here?

"M'lady, I've come to rescue you." He closed the door and barred it.

What? Nay. What was his intention?

He set the candlestick on the mantel and faced her. He was a big man, his graying hair in a queue and his dark beard reaching halfway down his broad chest. He was more than twice her age but still strong and in fine health. One thing struck her as odd—his clothing and face were clean. He obviously had not fought alongside her clan.

"The battle did not go well for your clan," he said. "I'm here to protect you from the MacKenzie heathens."

"You didn't fight," she blurted, trying to figure him out.

He grinned. "Nay. I wasn't the one who took a MacKenzie hostage. I have no quarrel with them. Why should I risk my life for your daft brother's sake?"

"Where is Elrick?"

"Dead."

"What?" She felt stunned for a moment, unsure how she felt about that. Though she loved her brother, as she did any family member, he had been cruel to her the last several months. And her jaw still ached from where he'd struck her. Most importantly, who would lead the clan? "How many died?" she asked.

"I know not, but have no fears. I still intend to make you my wife... after we wait and see if you're carrying a MacKenzie bastard."

Saints! What if she was carrying Shamus' bairn? A startling combination of joy and fear sliced through her, taking her breath away. More than anything, she wished to be with him and have a family together.

Whether she was with child or not, she would never willingly marry Sleat. Immersed in a real life nightmare, she shook her head.

Sleat frowned, his face darkening. "What is this? Are you refusing?"

"Aye. I don't wish to marry you."

"That whoreson Elrick lied to me," Sleat said, then shrugged. "Marriage is not necessary for what I want anyway." He moved toward her.

"Nay." She backed toward the window, trying to think of a solution... or what she could use as a weapon. The stoneware jug was on the opposite side of the bed. "Stay away from me!"

"I've been watching you, lass, and I want you under me at least once." He crept forward, a malicious grin on his face. "Aye, 'twill be a great pleasure to plow your meadow, even if I'm not the first. You little whore."

Her *sgian dubh*! It was strapped to her ankle. She would stab the bastard.

Pretending to cower, she crouched in the darkness behind her bed, reached down to her ankle and slid the small knife from the scabbard.

When he bent down, grasped her shoulders in his large, strong hands and lifted her, she stabbed the blade up into his gut. He growled like an enraged monster, shook her and threw her onto the bed. As he was grabbing for her weapon, something cracked and he fell on her like a massive sack of grain.

She glanced up to see Anora holding an iron fire poker over her head, her terrified eyes wide.

Maili shoved the dead weight of Sleat off her and scrambled from the bed. "Oh thank you, Anora! You knocked him out cold." She embraced her trembling maid. "I'm proud of you. You are truly a female warrior."

Anora dropped the poker and sobbed against Maili's shoulder. "M'lady. I couldn't let him do that to you."

"I thank you. You saved my life." Maili didn't think Sleat would've let her live after raping her. He would've pretended one of the invading MacKenzies did the evil deed, or one of Elrick's boorish guards. Obviously, Sleat had only been marrying her so he could drag her to his bed, whether she wished it or not.

"Come, let's quit this place afore he awakes." Maili urged Anora out of the room and locked the door.

They raced down the stairs as the first of dawn's light gleamed in the east. Though she was fortunate to have escaped a horrible fate, her heart was heavy with dread about what she would find below in the great hall and the courtyard.

When she reached the bottom of the steps, a dark-haired stranger turned, then strode across the great hall toward her, his hand on his sheathed sword hilt. Spattered and smeared blood covered him. A MacKenzie. She froze, but as he came closer she saw his resemblance to Shamus, though his eyes were lighter in color.

He glanced down at her clothing. "Are you Lady Maili?"

"Aye."

"Shamus is asking for you."

Concerned, she glanced about the hall, seeing several people, but not Shamus. "Where is he? Is he well?"

"Nay, he was badly injured in the fighting."

Icy fear drove through her. "Nay," she whispered in denial. "I must see him."

The man nodded. "I'm Dermott. Shamus is my brother. I'll take you to him. He has called out your name several times."

"Saints." Tears pricking her eyes, she quickened her steps. "Is the healer with him?"

"Aye. The MacKenzie healer." As they crossed the hall, Dermott asked, "Did someone hit you?"

His question startled her, for she could think of naught but Shamus. "What?"

"A large bruise covers your cheek and jaw."

"Oh, aye." She stroked her fingers over the sore spot the size of Elrick's fist. "But I'll be fine. 'Tis Shamus I'm most concerned about."

"I thank you for taking him food while your brother had him imprisoned."

She nodded, knowing she could've done naught else.

She entered the guest chamber where Shamus lay. Strangers, whom she assumed were his clansmen, stood along the walls. Another man was sewing up a bleeding cut on Shamus' abdomen. Was he the MacKenzie healer?

When she looked at Shamus' face, a fresh wave of cold fear washed over her. "Saints, he is so pale," Maili whispered.

"He lost a lot of blood," Dermott said behind her.

A melee of confused thoughts and sharp emotions spun within her. Could she use her "sight" to see if he would heal? Should she pray? Uncertain, she sat in the wooden chair by the bed and took his hand. "Shamus?" Her voice caught on his name and she leaned toward him. "'Tis me."

"Maili," he whispered, his hand tightening around hers. "Hurt?"

"Nay. I am well." She smoothed his hair back from his forehead. "But you are hurt badly."

"'Tis naught," he whispered, then took a shallow breath.

"Are you in a lot of pain?"

He remained silent, seeming to have fallen asleep. His breathing grew deep and even and she prayed he was truly resting so that he might heal. One of her clansmen, 'haps even her own brother, had done him grievous harm. Another bloody bandage was wrapped around his muscular upper arm. A multitude of blue and purple bruises covered most of his chest, ribs, and abdomen. Dear heavens! That was where her brother and his men had beaten him the night before.

"Is that her?" a deep voice asked behind her.

Maili turned to see a large, commanding warrior with midnight hair and dark brown eyes. A far more frightening version of Shamus.

"Aye, this is Lady Maili." Dermott motioned toward her.

"M'lady." The man gave a brief bow. "I am Cyrus, the MacKenzie chief." His voice seemed too loud for this small room.

Of course. How could he be anyone else? He had the same dangerous presence she had sensed in her visions.

Releasing Shamus' hand, she arose from the chair and curtseyed. "M'laird."

He eyed her curiously. "I've been told you helped my brother."

"Aye."

"You brought him food and helped him escape," he said in a matter-of-fact tone.

She nodded, feeling the urge to lower her gaze from his intimidating one, but she did not.

"I thank you," he said. "I owe you a debt of gratitude."

Behind her, Shamus uttered words and she turned to him. "What did you say?" She leaned down toward him and stroked his beard-roughened cheek.

He fell silent, appearing to be sleeping.

She sat on the chair again and held his hand. *Please, God, help him to heal and recover. I have not known him long but I know he is a good man. The only man for me.*

Moments later, someone tugged gently on her sleeve. "Pray pardon," Lettie, one of the maids whispered. "M'lady, the clan elders wish to speak to you."

Annoyed that someone would ask her to leave Shamus' side, she frowned. "Now?"

"Aye, they told me to find you and bring you to the solar. 'Tis urgent."

Though she didn't wish to be away from Shamus even for a minute, she knew she had to help her clan. "I will return soon, Shamus," she whispered and kissed his forehead. Reluctantly, she let go of his hand, praying he would be improved by the time she returned. "I'll be in the solar for a few minutes. If anything should change, please send someone to get me right away," she told Dermott.

He nodded.

Why did the elders wish to speak to her so soon? She did not even know how many of her clan were dead or injured yet.

In the solar, she closed the door behind her, then sat down at the table, surrounded by six clan elders, all men. Their long, bearded faces and reddened eyes showed the utter grief they felt at the loss of so many clan and family members.

"The MacKenzies have near destroyed the whole of our clan, lass," the ancient warrior, Hugh, growled. His gnarled hand clenched into a fist upon the table. "I do not ken whether we can survive this."

"How many died?" she asked.

"Five and twenty, our chief among them. With three more gravely injured."

Good Lord. So many? How could their clan endure such a great defeat? Her throat tightened, and tears burned her eyes.

"But 'twas no more than Elrick asked for when he took the MacKenzie lad hostage," her great uncle Bhatar said, his voice rough and raspy.

"I agree," Maili said, forcing her emotions aside, "and I saw this devastation in my visions. I warned Elrick but he would not listen to me."

The men nodded. "He refused to heed our council as well."

"We have sent three men after Neacal," Bhatar said. "We pray he is still living in the crofter's cottage on *Eilean Fraoch Dubh*."

Indeed, she hoped so, too.

Hugh frowned, his bushy white brows forming a V. "I told them not to send for him. He'll make a terrible chief. He's half mad. He could lose his sanity and kill the rest of the clan."

The other men grumbled their disagreement.

Maili's heart ached for her tormented brother. "Neacal has never killed anyone outside of battle."

"But you must admit, lass, that he is half mad."

Truly not believing he was, she shook her head.

"The men have said he was tortured. 'Twas almost more than his mind could withstand. Any of us might end up the same way if we were tortured."

Three of them nodded.

Hugh remained unmoved. "Still, I'm nay certain he will be the best leader for the clan."

"Who else then?" she asked.

"Three good candidates were killed in the siege," Kendrew said, his long white beard swaying as he looked back and forth at his comrades.

"Neacal has a different nature than Elrick," she said, hoping and praying her brother was able to be chief.

They all nodded.

"He has a good heart and he is intelligent."

"What if he doesn't wish to be chief?" Uncle Bhatar asked.

"Then I suppose he'll not return with the men you sent." If that was the case, what would happen to her clan?

CHAPTER ELEVEN

When Chief MacDonald of Sleat was found around noon, locked in Maili's bedchamber with a large knot on his head and a stab wound to his abdomen, he made up a story about being knocked on the head during battle, stabbed, and then dragged to her chamber. He claimed to hardly remember it. She would've had him removed earlier, but with everything that was going on, she'd forgotten about him.

Dermott stopped her in a corner of the great hall. "Is what Sleat said true?"

"Nay. He tried to force himself on me, and I defended myself," she whispered, not wanting to mention Anora for fear a maid might get into trouble for bashing the head of a chief. Maili did not know why but she felt more comfortable telling Dermott than anyone else, since Shamus was so ill. He then relayed the information to the others.

Cyrus MacKenzie consulted with the MacDonald clan elders, then told Sleat and his men to leave and never return. The chief was lucky to escape with only two minor injuries.

The next three days were a dark, exhausting blur for Maili. Her emotions were in turmoil. Not only was Shamus horribly injured and unresponsive much of the time because of blood loss, but the clan also held funerals for the twenty-five men who were killed during the battle, her brother's being the most elaborate. Her heart ached with the loss of so many of her fellow clansmen's brothers, fathers and sons in the battle. Their clan was forever changed and nearly decimated because of her daft brother's greed. Her emotions switched from sadness to anger so quickly she was shocked at herself. She would strangle Elrick if he wasn't already dead.

The MacKenzies had lost four men in the battle. After the clan held brief funerals for them, Cyrus sent a galley crew to take their bodies home to their families.

Tensions between the MacKenzies and MacDonalds were high but, to her relief, no fights broke out. Most of the MacKenzies' large force of soldiers camped on the hill above the castle, but Shamus' brothers and their personal guards remained inside the castle. She did not fear them and they treated her with what seemed to be genuine kindness. Many in her clan wished to kill the MacKenzies, but made no move to do so. They well knew they were outnumbered. Besides, the MacKenzies had disarmed them and imprisoned the most militant in the dungeon. She thought this was wise, because most of the men were Elrick's closest personal guard and they held the same mindset that Elrick had.

Late at night, Maili sat by Shamus' bedside holding his hand and willing him to awaken. Everyone else had retired to their beds. She hated the dark, dismal feeling that closed in around her. She had lost so many in her family and clan. She could not lose Shamus, too. Her second sight was proving no help to her now. She couldn't even get a glimmer of the future.

"Please, God, allow him to be by my side for a while longer, for a lifetime if it be your will," she whispered barely louder than a breath. "I haven't known him long, but I love him and I know our souls are bound."

Tears streamed down her face and blurred her vision, almost causing her to miss the movement of his head.

He inhaled a deep, audible breath. "Maili?"

Gasping, she wiped her tears away. "I am here." She leaned toward him.

He opened his eyes a crack and focused on her in the candlelight. "How many days have I lain abed?"

"Three. How do you feel?" She stroked a hand along his dark-whiskered jaw.

He frowned. "What the devil happened to your face? You have an enormous bruise. Were you injured in the battle?"

"Nay." She touched her fingertips to the tender skin of her cheek where she knew the bruise was turning from purple to disgusting shades of green and yellow. "Elrick struck me with his fist after the garrison brought us back that day."

"That whoreson," Shamus said through clenched teeth. "I'm not sorry I killed him now."

Maili was surprised, but not angered or hurt by his admission. "Oh. You... were the one who killed him?"

"Aye, in the skirmish. He fought hard, but I finally managed to gain the upper hand."

"Was he the one who gave you these sword wounds?" she asked.

"Nay, 'twas another of your clansmen. In truth, I'm sorry if the loss of your brother pains you, but he got no more than he deserved."

She nodded, saddened that her brother had not been a better person. "I agree. He was too brutal and callous."

Shamus gazed at her solemnly and she squeezed his hand. "How do you feel?" she asked.

"Not as bad as before." His expression lightened and a wee smile lifted one corner of his lips.

She smiled back, wishing she could kiss him. "Thanks be to God. I have some broth for you." She retrieved the wooden bowl from the hearth where it had been kept warm.

"Nay, I cannot stomach it," he grumbled.

"You must eat to regain your strength."

"Och. Very well. One sip."

Using the wooden spoon, she eased the broth into his mouth.

After he swallowed, he said, "I must speak to you about something important."

"Aye, what is it?" She placed the bowl on the table, sat by his side again and grasped his hand.

"If I survive this... will you marry me?"

Joy burst through her and tears of happiness pricked her eyes. "Of course, I will. And you will survive."

"I believe you," he said, studying her intently, "for you have the sight, do you not?"

Sudden fear crushed her happiness and seized her breath. If he knew the truth, would he withdraw his proposal?

"Why do you not want me to know about your gift?" he asked gently.

"I fear... that you will not want me if you think me a witch."

"Nonsense, *mo graibh*. Second sight is not the same as witchcraft." He gazed at her with such affection it near broke her heart. "I love you, Maili. No matter what."

Her throat tightened and tears of gratitude and happiness flowed from her eyes. "And I love you."

"Shh, don't cry. I vow to make you happy." He brought her hand to his mouth and kissed it. "Are you certain your clan will allow us to marry?"

She dried her eyes. "Aye, I believe they will." She lowered her voice to a whisper. "After all, you have compromised me."

He sent her a broad grin. "Aye, and I cannot wait to do that again, m'lady."

Her face heated. "Then you must eat and grow strong."

"Aye, I believe I'll have another sip of that broth now." After he had drunk a bit more, he grew serious again. "Who will lead your clan now?"

"Some of my clansmen have taken a galley out to the isle to find my other brother. We're praying he will want to be chief."

Four days later, Shamus had improved enough to join everyone in the great hall for supper. She had helped him bathe, shave and put on clean clothing. The food had just been served at the high table when the entry door burst open. Her brother Neacal strode in, followed by his wolfhound and the three clansmen who had gone to get him.

She had not seen him in several months, since their father's funeral. His windblown dark hair had grown long, past his shoulders, and he had not shaved in a great while. His wild blue eyes, the same color as her own, scanned those in the great hall, slashing sharply over the MacKenzies.

She arose and strode across the large room toward him. She had not remembered the pink scar on his handsome face being so pronounced. Knowing the pain and torture he must have suffered, her heart broke yet again. "Neacal, I'm so glad you've come."

"I need to speak with you in private," he murmured.

"Of course. Are you hungry?"

"Nay."

Although she suspected he was lying, for he was much leaner than the last time she'd seen him, she proceeded to the library and he followed with his dog, then closed the door.

"What the devil happened here?" he demanded. "The MacKenzies killed Elrick and half our clan, and now they feast in our great hall?"

She held up her hand. "After a galley wreck, Shamus MacKenzie washed up on shore nearby. Elrick and his men beat him severely, then threw him in the dungeon. Our brother believed he could get a great deal of money from the MacKenzie chief. Instead of bringing ransom, he laid siege to the place. You would've done the same if your brother had been taken hostage."

"Whose side are you on?" His piercing blue eyes burned into her.

"Do you wish the truth?"

"Aye. Never lie to me, sister."

She took a deep breath. "The truth is... I love Shamus MacKenzie and I intend to marry him."

Neacal's eyes widened and he cursed. "Are you mad?"

"Nay. He is a good man. He did naught wrong. Elrick and his men beat him black and blue twice. If not for me taking him food, Elrick would've let him starve in the dungeon."

Neacal shook his head, looking weary and tired. "I feared the power would go to Elrick's head."

"It did."

Her brother stared out at the loch below for several moments.

"Will you stay and become the chief?" she asked quietly.

He turned his turbulent gaze upon her. "I was never meant to be chief."

"I ken with a certainty you will make a far better one than Elrick."

"I will do what is best for the clan. 'Tis what Da would ask of me, and I can do no less."

At his words of self-sacrifice, her heart squeezed and ached. How could her two brothers be so different? "Da would be so proud of you, Neacal. You're a good man, and I pray you will find peace and happiness."

He gave a brief humorless laugh and glanced away. "Not in this life, Maili. But my happiness is of no import. Like I said, I'll do what is best for the clan." He appeared resigned to his fate... and miserable.

"Is there anything I can do to help you?"

"Nay. Knowing I have your approval is enough. If you're going to marry the MacKenzie man, you'll be leaving us, aye?"

"'Tis true. Not that I wish to leave you or my clan," she said, sadness weighing upon her. "I will come to visit often."

He nodded, looking troubled. "Near half the men of the clan are dead at the MacKenzies' hand. I'll have to hire guards. And 'tis obvious our defenses require shoring up if the MacKenzies overtook the castle so easily."

"They're highly trained warriors. And if you're going to blame anyone for this disaster, blame Elrick."

He nodded again. "He made a bad choice and then underestimated them."

A knock sounded at the door.

Maili opened it and found Shamus standing just outside with his younger brother Fraser. Entering, Shamus took her hand and kissed the back. Warmth and affection spread through her. She introduced her brother to the MacKenzies and held her breath until Neacal offered his hand and they shook.

"We wish to speak to your brother alone for a few moments," Shamus said.

Her face heated when she realized Shamus planned to ask for her hand in marriage.

Her eyes wide, Maili sent Shamus a wee grin, nodded and exited the room. He adored her blushes and enchanting smiles.

He eyed the man across from him, about his own size, lean and muscular. He looked as if he'd been training intensely. Though the man's eyes were the same color as his sister's, the expression in them was completely different. The man possessed a feral, unpredictable quality that put him on edge. Fraser had insisted on accompanying Shamus since he was not yet fully recovered.

"I'm sorry for what happened between our clans," Shamus said, hoping Maili's wild-eyed brother would not throw a dirk at him.

"And I'm sorry Elrick took you hostage."

"I want you to know, I love Lady Maili and I want to ask for your permission to marry her."

Neacal eyed him critically. "Very well. 'Tis what she wishes. I hope this marriage will forge an alliance between our clans so we'll have no more violence between us."

Shamus nodded. "I'm certain my brother Cyrus, the chief, will be glad to hear this."

Maili had never been happier than when she married Shamus the following week in her family's wee chapel beside the castle. The light from a multitude of candles pierced the gloaming and reflected off the stained glass windows. Tears of joy blurred her vision as Shamus vowed to cherish and honor her through this life and into the next. After she repeated her vows, they were pronounced man and wife. Shamus smiled, leaned down and gave her a kiss filled with love and devotion.

They ran through the rain to the great hall where a grand wedding feast awaited them.

Though Shamus' brothers had teased him mercilessly with plenty of gibes about being a married man and, in effect, still a prisoner, he smiled, ignored them and fed her bites of venison, bread and cheese from their shared trencher. She had never known such bliss was possible.

A traveling band of minstrels had arrived on a galley the day before and were now entertaining them from an elevated platform in the far corner of the great hall. When a new ballad began, the hauntingly beautiful female voice floating through the air caught Maili's attention. Except for the singer's voice, a hush fell over the large room. Everyone paused to listen and search out the owner. But in the dimness of the corner, 'twas impossible to make out many details of the lass.

"Saints," Neacal hissed softly, sitting beside Maili.

She glanced at him to find him transfixed, a look of awe on his face such as she'd never before seen.

It seemed everyone held their breaths until the song ended. After a great applause resounded to the rafters, the musicians launched into a lively instrumental gig and everyone resumed eating and talking.

Around midnight, when their clansmen were busy drinking and dancing, Maili and Shamus slipped away from the *céilidh*. Once in her decorated, candlelit bedchamber, Shamus said, "We should've returned to the standing stones for our wedding night."

She snickered. "Are you mad? The rain is pouring down out there."

He grinned. "Aye, mad for you." He slid his arms around her waist, drew her to him and kissed her. She was indeed thankful he was near fully recovered and gaining more strength each day.

When he stripped the clothing from her body, she was glad for the cozy fire in the hearth. Moments later, they were both naked beneath the bedcovers, her body tight against his.

She sighed and pulled him closer. "This is far better than the hard ground."

"Aye." He placed cherishing kisses over her face and down her neck, then lifted up to look into her eyes. "I love you, Maili, and I'm so happy I found you. The galley wreck, beatings, injuries and imprisonment were worth it."

Tears burning her eyes, she shook her head, unable to comprehend all he'd endured. "I'm sorry you went through all that pain. But I'm glad you found me here. No one could ever make me as happy as you do." And truly, she had never been as happy as she was at this moment. "In my heart, I married you that night at the standing stones."

"Aye, I should've realized the same thing, but you are far wiser than I am, my wee fairy lass."

He gave her a soul-deep kiss and she could think no more. Her full attention was on the love that wrapped them in a warm embrace and the hot, delectable sensations he showered upon her.

EPILOGUE

The sky was clear blue the next morn when the MacKenzies, including Shamus, Maili and her maid, Anora, boarded galleys to head north to Teasairg Castle. Though Maili was sad to leave her brother and her clan, she was excited to find a new home with Shamus.

After embracing Neacal, she said, "I truly do hope you will be content here, brother."

"I'll do my best." His stormy gaze searched hers. "But more importantly, I hope you'll be happy with your new husband and the MacKenzies."

"I'm certain I will. Shamus is a good man."

Neacal nodded. "Send word to me if he becomes otherwise," he said dryly.

She let a small grin slip out. "I don't think that will happen."

Moments later, she bid her brother and her clan farewell and the MacKenzie warriors shoved the eight galleys into the loch. Maili had always enjoyed riding in a galley and loved it even more with Shamus at her side.

A fair wind pushed them north at a great pace, and by sunset they were sailing up a beautiful loch. Sunlight played through the mist and clouds as the galleys glided smoothly through the water.

"This is Loch Alsh," Shamus said. "And there is your new home, Teasairg Castle." He pointed at a tall gray structure in the far distance she could barely make out.

As they drew nearer, she could see that the castle, surrounded by high walls, sat upon a small island.

"'Tis lovely," she said.

"You are the one who is lovely." He slipped his hand into her hair and kissed her lips.

"Control yourself, man," Fraser said behind them. "Only a few more minutes and the honeymoon can begin."

"The honeymoon has already begun," Shamus retorted.

The men around them laughed.

Grinning, Maili covered her burning face with her hands. But in truth, her blood heated when she realized how much she looked forward to joining Shamus in his bed this night.

"I believe I'll hold you captive in my bedchamber for a month or two," Shamus whispered into her ear.

"I shall be your willing prisoner."

Thank you for picking up my book. If you enjoyed it, please consider leaving a short review to help other readers determine if the book is right for them. To learn about my upcoming releases, please sign up for my newsletter at my website: www.vondasinclair.com.

HIGHLAND ADVENTURE SERIES

My Fierce Highlander (Alasdair and Gwyneth)
My Wild Highlander (Lachlan and Angelique)
My Brave Highlander (Dirk and Isobel)
My Daring Highlander (Keegan and Seona)
My Notorious Highlander (Torrin and Jessie)
My Rebel Highlander (Rebbie and Calla)
My Captive Highlander (Shamus and Maili)
Highlander Unbroken (Neacal and Anna)
Highlander Entangled (Colin and Kristina)

SCOTTISH TREASURE SERIES

Stolen by a Highland Rogue (Dugald and Camille)
Defended by a Highland Renegade (Mairiana and Darack)

More stories will be coming soon!

ABOUT THE AUTHOR

Vonda Sinclair is the *USA Today* bestselling author of award-winning Scottish historical romance. Her favorite pastime is exploring Scotland and taking photos along the way. She also enjoys creating hot, Highland heroes and spirited, unconventional lasses to drive them mad. She lives in the mountains of North Carolina where she is crafting another Scottish story. Please visit her website at: www.vondasinclair.com

www.ingramcontent.com/pod-product-compliance
Lightning Source LLC
LaVergne TN
LVHW090631120126
829613LV00006B/131